A HISTORY OF SARCASM

FRANK BURTON

Dog Horn Publishing
6 Athlone Terrace
Armley
Leeds
LS12 1UA
United Kingdom

Printed in the United Kingdom.

Edited by Jill Morris.
Typeset by Adam Lowe.

ACKNOWLEDGEMENTS:

My work has appeared previously in the following publications: *Aabehlpt, Joost* and *A History of Sarcasm* in *Etchings*; *The Day She Melted* and *Voom and Bloom* in *Polluto*; *The Opening* in *The Beat*; *The Wondering* in *Twisted Tongue*; *Walter Walks Sideways* in *Skive Quarterly*; and *The Point* on laurahird.com. *The World* was broadcast on BBC Radio 4's *Opening Lines* programme in April 2009.

Thanks to everyone who has helped to promote and develop my fiction over the last few years. Special thanks to Adam Lowe, Jill Morris, Dave Swann, Kef F. Sutherland, Claire Nixon, Matt Ward, Peter Tennant, Laura Hird, Gemma Jenkins, Patrick Allington, Sabina Hopfer, Dave Ansell, Oliver Mann, Dave Hailwood, Jon Clatworthy, Andy Kempson, Dom Collis, Patrick Marriott, Lee Kierons, Anthony Lye, Dave Insley and Simon May. Thanks to Priya for the love and support.

To my dad

CONTENTS

FOREWORD

If I was a character in this impressive debut collection, I'd probably start by quoting a few authoritative-sounding facts about the author.

To the best of my knowledge, I'm *not* a character in any of these stories, but I'm going to do that anyway. Because there is a refreshing Mark E. Smith-style contrary streak running throughout *A History of Sarcasm*, and I want to stay true to it.

So here goes.

Frank Burton was born to Bulgarian parents in a shed in the village of Heaven, on the border between Sussex and Lancashire. The village is bisected by two minor lay-lines, and famous for its award-winning Museum of Sieves and Colanders. Frank Burton has remained in the shed ever since, although it is now underneath a Tesco's store.

Clearly, very little of the above is true, but I feel able to begin in this manner because it fits with some of the themes in this collection – namely: lies, God, the paranormal, people getting buried under things, invented biographies, and sieves.

(Only one of the items in the above list is made up, although I refuse to identify which one it is, since the characters in this book usually stick to their guns, particularly when they know it will end badly for them if they persist with their fantasies or when the lie is all they've got left to believe in).

I guess, at this point, I should tell you what I like about this book, and why you should read it.

First, it made me laugh out loud in places. Second, it's well written (the characters are often out of control, but the prose is steely and precise). Third, it sometimes gave me the feeling I was falling.

If you've ever been lucky enough to get that sense of vertigo in writers like Borges, Carol Shields, Roberto Bolano, Thomas Pynchon, Michel Butor, or Kurt Vonnegut, then you'll know what I'm on about.

If you don't – as one of Burton's characters might say – well, I'm not that bothered. Just leave it, OK?

Just leave it.

◘

I left a pause there because that's what sometimes happens in Frank's book when characters come back to themselves after gazing down into literature's dizzying void or worrying themselves to a stand-still about the weirdness of the words that they've somehow conjured in their mouths.

The writer William Burroughs once called language "a virus from outer space", and there's a sense of that in *A History of Sarcasm*, where Burton holds words up to the sun and lets the light shine through them (until so much light floods through that the words are bleached out completely).

The other two things I should tell you about this book are:

1. It's easy to read.
3. You'll sometimes feel like you're going mad when you read it, particularly during the scary, hilarious labyrinth of 'Multiple Stories'.
C. It contains lists that aren't always to be trusted, and which are often rooted in paranoia and Obsessive Compulsive Disorders.
2. At times you'll be moved, particularly by a relatively straightforward little gem called 'The Point' which ends with a twang that still resonating in my chest (I was going to say 'heart', but one of Burton's characters would probably have tutted at me). 'The Point' is soaked in authentic emotion yet balanced by steely control, and it points to one of the future directions that this fascinating debutant might take.

Because that's the last thing to say: Frank Burton is still the trendy side of 30. And if you get into the sickeningly young man's work while he's still in the early stages of infancy, you'll experience that pleasurable glow known by teenagers who are the first to discover a band destined for greatness.

This probably means you'll have gone off Frank's work by the time he's become The Godfather of the New Slipstream in British Fiction and he's shooting off his mouth from the top of a pile of gold bullion.

But he probably won't be that bothered because he'll be sitting on top of a pile of gold bullion.

Or, at least, some future version of him might be.

In fact, if this *was* a Burton story, this is where we'd probably start: with a future version of Frank Burton sitting on some bullion, fretting that he's simply the product of a daydream by a young writer, who's imagining the glorious career that is to come.

Perhaps the fretting future version of Frank would then do the most logical thing that writers do when faced by this kind of existential crisis.

He'd invent an authentic-sounding academic to write an authentic-sounding foreword about his work.

If you see what I mean.

But if you don't – as one of Frank Burton's characters might say – then that's OK too, mate.

All right?

'David Swann',
English Department,
The University of Chichester,
April, 2009

AABEHLPT
(A List)

A

It always begins with **A**. The first, greatest and most powerful of all letters. It is the first letter of the word "alphabet" as well as the first letter of my pseudonym, Adam.

My friend Annie has advised me on a number of occasions that I ought to compile a list of things that I alphabetise on a day-to-day basis. For some reason she seems to think that if I put it all down on paper it will make me realise how "ridiculous" my perfectly sensible organisational processes are.

Still, I am not doing this for her benefit. I am doing this simply because I like to alphabetise. To be frank, I am ashamed I never thought of it myself.

B
Books

Of course, plenty of people alphabetise their books. However, my collection is extra special, as not only are the volumes on my shelf arranged in an alphabetised order, they are also alphabetised in content. I have an aversion to books that are not structured A–Z, which unfortunately means that I am unable to read anything other than reference books. My collection begins with the *A–Z* and finishes with *Who's Who*. Don't get me wrong, I'd be happy to read a novel one day if authors of fiction began organising themselves efficiently.

C
CD Collection

I believe this is also common. Annie herself admits to having an alphabetised CD collection, although when I visited her flat to inspect it, I found it to be nothing of the kind.

"This is not an alphabetised CD collection," I told her.

"Why not?" she asked.

"Well, for one thing, you've only alphabetised by artist and not by album title. Look at this Beatles section. You've put *Abbey Road* way ahead of all these other ones."

"They're placed in the order in which they were recorded," she said. "Is that a problem?"

"Well, it's your system, I suppose," I said.

"I'd be interested to know, actually, whereabouts under your system you would place *The White Album*."

"Well, that's easy, because it's not actually called *The White Album*, it's eponymous. I would place it under B for 'Beatles'."

"So, you wouldn't put it under T for 'The Beatles'?"

"No, the listing would appear, 'Beatles, The'. But you can make your own rules regarding 'the' and 'a' and suchlike. That's the beauty of it."

I am not sure she understood the beauty of it.

D
Dinner

I eat my food in alphabetical order. If I am having soup as a starter, that usually has to be eaten after the main course, unless the main course is something slightly higher up the chain, like spaghetti. By the same rules, if I am having cake for desert, quite often I have to eat desert first. There are also occasions when I have to eat desert halfway through a meal. If I have a glass of wine with the meal, that usually has to wait until last. It is for this reason that I never participate in toasting at weddings, unless it is after food.

E
Everything

This isn't strictly true, although I wish it were. I only include this as an entry here as Annie accuses me of doing so all the time: "Adam, you alphabetise *everything*!"

Maybe one day, with enough hard work and effort.

F
Food (see D: **Dinner**)

The food in my cupboard is alphabetised according to type rather than brand name. For example, in my condiments section, Branston pickle is placed after Heinz ketchup, because if I happen to buy another brand of pickle one day, this too will be placed under P for pickle. Once I have unpacked my shopping and alphabetised it, I then proceed to place the carrier bags in my alphabetised carrier bag drawer. Here, in contrast to the food cupboards, I have decided to sort according to the name of the store where I purchased the bags—Asda, B&Q, Costcutter, and so on. This is the only way to avoid any confusion.

G
Grapes (see F: **Food**)
This is only a minor category, as there are only ever four kinds of grape in my kitchen—green seeded, green seedless, red seeded, red seedless. It is a rare occasion that all four are present at any one time, although it is worth noting that even if there is only one type of grape in my kitchen, it does not mean that the grapes are not alphabetised. It simply means that the list is very short.

H
History
A number of the historical encyclopaedias in my collection have timelines at the beginning. I have reordered these, producing what I call "Time Zigzags" on my computer, detailing each event in its proper order. I have printed them out and pasted them over top of the original timelines.

Time Zigzags are much more in keeping with my own personal view of history. On a conventional timeline, the English Civil War appears after the Renaissance. This, to me, is clearly wrong. What does it matter what year a particular event took place? It is in the past; finished. This does not mean we shouldn't alphabetise them for posterity, of course.

There are some historical events that appear at roughly the same position on both a timeline and a Time Zigzag—the World Wars, for example—but this is pure coincidence.

Time Zigzags are probably my second-favourite alphabetising scheme. As far as I know, no one else has ever had such a notion, and frankly, I cannot see why not. It only occurred to me after completing them that their crisscrossed lines appear to resemble the display on a heart monitor—a sure sign that I have my "finger on the pulse".

I
Instructions

Not being the most technically minded person, I often have to consult the instructions for my computer. These are filed neatly into the C section of my collected instructions. Now, some might ask, if I use these instructions on a regular basis, why don't I keep them out on the desk next to my computer? Indeed, Annie posed this very question recently.

"Well, for one thing," I said, "I might lose them. That isn't the only reason, but it's a fundamental truth that things left lying around will go astray, unless they are kept in some kind of order."

"Hence the alphabetising," she said.

"And what is that supposed to mean?" I said.

"I think you alphabetise things in order to stop yourself from losing anything."

"As I say, that is one factor . . ."

"I don't mean to get too deep here," she said, "but could it be something to do with losing your parents when you were young?"

"Don't be stupid," I said. "To 'lose' someone is just a figure of speech that people use to avoid the word 'death'. My parents *died*. I didn't *lose* them."

"I know, I know," she said, "but maybe you still feel guilty about it."

"I didn't kill them," I said.

"No, no, I'm not saying you did. What I'm saying is . . ."

"What you're saying is you think I'm obsessed. Perhaps I am, but isn't everybody obsessed with something? You seem to be obsessed with me and my obsessions."

"Somebody's got to be."

I am not entirely sure what she meant.

J
Jumpers

These are filed according to the predominant colour. Jumpers with patterns on them that do not have one predominant colour are filed under M for "Mixed". Jumpers in the Mixed section are then filed according to the two most prominent colours. For example, "Blue, Black" comes before "Blue, Grey".

K
Keyboard

I have reordered the keys on my keyboard to replace the nonsensical QWERTYUIOP etc. with the far more pleasing and user-friendly ABCDEFGHIJ. To be frank, I do not know what the manufacturers were thinking. I have also tried my best to alphabetise the punctuation marks, although the technician who reordered my keyboard for me said he could do nothing about the fact that colon and semi-colon are included on the same key. This made me very angry. It's a jump of sixteen whole letters! I later reassured myself that a semi-colon could realistically be filed under C, as after all, it is a type of colon. I'm still not very happy about this, but I try not to think about it too much.

L
Laundry

Don't even get me started on laundry. For an insight into a typical laundry day, see notes under **J: Jumpers**. The same general rules apply to each article of clothing, but of course they need to be filed by type first. Laundry days are by far the longest of my week, and can at times be a genuine test of faith in the whole system.

I don't want to talk about laundry.

M
Money

I have created a series of small pockets in my wallet for small change to be sorted according to its alphabetical rather than numerical value: Fifty Pence, Five Pence, One Pence, One Pound, Ten Pence, Twenty Pence, Two Pence, Two Pounds. In a conventional alphabetised list, these coins would be ordered according to the value of the number. However, I have always been opposed to this tradition of placing numbers before letters in an alphabetised list, somehow suggesting that numerical figures are more worthy of our attention.

That said, I do acknowledge that mine is a controversial view, and certainly do not begrudge any individual who decides to order their coins numerically. It is, after all, probably a little easier that way.

N
Neapolitan ice-cream
I prefer to eat Neapolitan ice cream in alphabetical order, chocolate first, then strawberry, followed by vanilla. This is a very difficult task, and requires me to separate each flavour into a separate bowl, disposing of any parts in which two flavours have mingled together. Often, by the time this task is completed, the ice cream has already melted. I have recently stopped purchasing Neapolitan ice cream, as I have come to the conclusion that it is a lot simpler to purchase individual flavours separately. Technically, therefore, Neapolitan ice cream should not be part of this list, but I have included it here, as I could not think of anything else that I alphabetise that starts with the letter N. Apologies.

O
Oranges
Unlike many other people, I am able to distinguish between various different types, and have arranged my oranges alphabetically from clementines through to tangerines. The only slight problem that remains is that I have never been able to distinguish adequately tangerines from satsumas. I suspect that they are one and the same fruit, but there remains a lingering doubt. The fact that the letters S

and T are alphabetical neighbours provides me with some small comfort.

P
People

I managed to upset Annie recently. We were having a particularly intimate conversation, in which she revealed some quite surprising facts about her childhood. We were sitting together on her bed, holding hands as we often would when having a heart to heart.

She hugged me, and thanked me for being there.

"I'm so glad you thought of calling me today, Adam," she said.

"I'm glad too," I said.

"You know you're my best friend, don't you?" she said. "I know I've only known you for a couple of years, Adam, but I think you're the best friend I've ever had. I really mean that."

"You're my best friend too," I said, and I also meant exactly what I said.

"What made you think of me today?" she said.

"I just wanted to talk to someone," I said. "Whenever I do, I always call you."

"My god, that is so sweet," she said. "God, Adam, I think I'm going to cry. We just have this great connection, don't we? And it's not like a sexual thing, or anything, it's like something more important than that."

"I agree," I said. "But really, you shouldn't think of it as 'sweet'."

"Why not?" she said.

"Well, you know how I like to alphabetise things?"

"Yes?"

"Your number is the first number in my phone, and it's also the first number in my address book. It's because your name begins with the letter A."

There was a long silence.

"It's your turn to speak," I said. "I said something, and then stopped talking, so that means that it's your go. You'd be rude not to."

"Rude?" she said. "*Rude?* Get out. Get out, now. I don't want to speak to you. Right now, I don't think I ever want to speak to you again."

Obediently, I left the room, and went to the hallway to put my shoes on.

Annie came after me.

"So that's really it?" she said. "That's the only reason we're such good friends? That's the only reason you called me today? Because my name appears first in your phone?"

"Yes," I said. "But for once, this isn't me and my so-called 'obsession'. Mobile phones automatically alphabetise names. Address books start with the letter A. It isn't me, it's *society*."

"Sort yourself out," she said. "Think about what it is that you're saying. I want you to go away now, and don't come back until you've realised that people are more important than *letters*."

But the fact of the matter is, I'm not sure that people *are* more important than letters. It's such an unfair comparison. When people die, it is sad, but society continues happily without them, almost as though they were never there in the first place. Conversely, if we lost one of the letters in the alphabet, everything would grind to a halt.

Q
Quick, Brown Fox Jumps Over A Lazy Dog, The
I would just like to take this opportunity to say that I hate this sentence. Is it supposed to be clever, or something?

R
Rubbish
I have several bins, for both recyclable and non-recyclable waste. This has proven to be a major problem, as there are many different items that need to be disposed of on a day-to-day basis, and it is simply not practical to have a separate bin for each of them. At one

point I had thirty-seven swing-top bins, many of which spent most of their time empty, as they were reserved for items that I do not normally use. I have recently revised this system in the interests of floor space. Whereas before I had a bin reserved specifically for banana skins, I now have a bin for all leftover fruit and veg. I used to have separate bins for newspapers, magazines and envelopes, but now I simply have a bin for wastepaper.

I would like to state categorically that I not in any way regard this revision as a defeat. Alphabetising is about being practical, and if something is not practical, it needs to be adjusted in order to make it so.

S
Stamps
If, indeed, Annie is right, and I "have a problem", perhaps this springs from the fact that my father was an obsessive stamp collector. I inherited his extensive stamp collection, and have since alphabetised it (a task that took several weeks), before locking it away, not intending to expand the collection any further.

I am interested in my father, but I am not interested in stamps, alphabetised or otherwise.

T
The
As I have already suggested, under my system, anything beginning with the word "The" should not be filed under the letter T, but under the first letter of the word following the word "The". I don't mean to repeat myself. I just wanted to make this point absolutely clear.

U
Underwear
See **J: Jumpers** for general clothing guidelines.

V
Vests
See above.

W
Words

Well, this is the big one, folks. My most radical idea to date, which has thus far attracted no adherents whatsoever. This does not necessarily mean that the idea is not a wonderful one. Alphabetising words effectively brings about a brand-new language, based closely on English, but resembling something else entirely. For example, a simple sentence such as "The cat sat on the mat," under my new system reads, "Eht act ast no eht amt." Admittedly, it is a difficult language to learn, not to mention pronounce, and requires a lot of dedication. At present, I am spending around four to five hours every day perfecting the art of what I like to call "Aabehlpt Aekps", or "Alphabet Speak", to give it its standard English name. I am now reaching a point that may almost be defined as fluent.

It's just a shame that I'm the only person who can actually speak the language.

X
Xylophone

I bought one especially for the purposes of compiling this list. Of course, the beauty of my xylophone is that its notes are already alphabetised without me having to lift a finger. Well, I suppose they would have been, had there only been one scale of notes instead of three. The notes on my xylophone now run A, A, A, B, B, B, and so on. It is still possible to play a coherent tune—it is simply a matter of observing the order in which the notes have been placed.

Y
Yoghurt

There is a particular type of yoghurt that I sometimes buy that has fruit in one section, and yoghurt in another. I am guessing that the manufacturers intended for people to mix the two together, but I find it a lot more pleasing to eat the fruit first. It doesn't matter what the fruit is, it will never beat the yoghurt in the race to finish last. Not unless there is a fruit out there that begins with the letter Z. I'm not sure that such a fruit currently exists.

Z
Zoo Animals

In a bid to make amends with Annie, I agreed to meet up with her at a neutral location, i.e. at neither of our homes. I suggested going for a coffee, but Annie insisted on a day out at the zoo. It is not a place that I would ordinarily visit, but considering the circumstances I chose not to refuse.

"So," she said as I arrived, "how are you?"

It had been several weeks since our little misunderstanding, and although we'd spoken several times on the phone, actually meeting her in person brought about a certain amount of tension, marked by the absence of any physical contact.

"Fine," I said.

"Look," she said, "thanks for coming. You know, for making the effort."

"I'm not sure that you'll like what I'm about to say next," I said, "but if it's OK with you, I'd like to wear a blindfold."

"Won't you miss all the animals?"

"You misunderstand. What I'd like to do is wear the blindfold in between the different sections in order to view the animals in alphabetical order. I've obtained a copy of the site map, and traced an appropriate route. So, if it's OK for you to guide me . . ."

She shrugged. "Whatever."

Being unable to see was not a comfortable experience, but if I was going to do this, I was determined to do it properly. I realised as we walked arm in arm that there was really only one person in the world that I could trust to accompany me in this manner. I felt safe with Annie, in the same way that I feel safe when I'm alone.

She raised her fingers to my face and removed the blindfold.

I opened my eyes.

She was smiling.

I returned the gesture, and looked beyond her over the nearby fence.

"What's that?" I said.

"It's a yak," she replied, rather proudly.

"I don't understand."

"Well, it was going to be a zebra, but they don't have any zebras."

"You did this deliberately?"

"Yes," she said. Her hand was on my back, stroking. "You see, here we are, two friends at the zoo, looking at a yak. And where's the harm in that? You're still alive."

"I didn't think I was going to die," I said. "I just prefer it . . ."

"You can't always get what you want though, Adam. Sometimes you have to accommodate for things that are beyond your control. *Most* of the time, in fact. It's what people do."

"It's not what I do."

"It should be," she said. "We all need to lose control every once in a while. You need *freedom*, Adam—you need to start breaking some of these self-imposed ruled and start *living*."

"I'm already alive, thanks."

"Look," she said, pointing to the yak.

I didn't look.

"It's an animal," she said. "A for Animal. The next one will also be an animal. If you can't bring yourself to break the rules, can't you *change* them at least?"

"Because they're all different animals, you stupid bitch."

The hand disappeared.

"I'm sorry, I can't do this any more."

I couldn't watch her walking away.

A part of me was glad she was gone. After all, those needless questions were running along behind her.

With hindsight, I'd like to think that I was right. However sincere her intentions, she remained wrong.

Better off without the aggravation.

Plenty more where she came from, anyway.

There's always Belinda.

THE ILLUSION OF SECURITY

Frisk works in security. The building he works in was once leased by a large insurance company, who employed him as a guard. Now the company, along with the rest of its staff, is gone. Frisk remains, supplying security for the owners of the building, ensuring it remains free from looters and squatters.

He works a twelve-hour shift, from midnight to twelve noon seven days a week. Long hours, but Frisk is the first to admit this is not exactly "work". Mainly, he sits and drinks in a small room on the ground floor, observing what remains of the CCTV installations. Surveillance cameras only cover around half of the building, the other half being either broken or disconnected as a means of saving electricity.

Tonight is a typical shift. Frisk arrives at work and exchanges pleasantries with Creek, who covers the daytimes.

"Alright, mate?"

"Alright. Anything?"

"Nothing."

They laugh, in recognition of the fact that they have this one identical conversation every night. They laugh every night, too, at its clockwork repetition.

Suddenly, the smile disappears from Creek's face, and Frisk can sense what's coming.

"There's been another one," says Creek. "Bloke on the bridge. Two of them knocked him out and chucked him in the river just for a loaf of bread in a carrier bag. Don't bear thinking about."

"No, it don't," says Frisk.

Frisk is always a little sceptical about these unsubstantiated tales. It's always a friend of a friend; someone who knows someone who saw something happen to someone else. In the absence of proper news reports, it's difficult to decide who to believe, even if the person telling the story believes it himself.

It's clear that Creek believes every word that he utters, but he was never the brightest spark. A nice enough guy, though. Good for a laugh. A bit of a practical joker, but Frisk can handle that. If he's honest with himself, he appreciates Creek's company enormously. If he's feeling brutally honest, he'll confess that Creek is the closest thing he has to a friend.

Frisk is separated from his wife and child, for a combination of personal and financial reasons. Under different circumstances, their split would've happened naturally sooner or later, as he and his wife were prone to harsh arguments. As Frisk would later reflect, they had little in common to begin with. In this sense, Frisk was almost grateful for the economic downturn that forced his wife and young daughter to live at the opposite end of the country, while he stayed on in the city on the promise of a steady wage. He sends them a portion of his money, and sometimes they speak on the phone when they can manage to get a connection.

When Creek has gone, Frisk goes for a walk up the stairs, and wanders around one of the offices on the third floor for a while before returning to the ground. He conducts a similar half-hearted patrol every evening, always resisting moving to the upper part of the building.

Both Frisk and Creek suspect that there have been people living in the upper floors for some time, although neither is prepared forcibly to evict them, partly through fear and partly out of sympathy. In any case, neither of them has actually seen these mystery intruders, as the cameras don't cover those particular floors. Now and again, there are indistinguishable shouts from above, which both Frisk and Creek choose to ignore.

There was one isolated incident a few weeks ago, when a chair came crashing through one of the eighth-floor windows, straight into the road. Frisk wasn't there at the time, but he's often replayed this rare moment of excitement back in his mind: the shower of broken glass, the flimsy plastic swivel seat busting in half on the concrete, its clatter echoing around the streets of the deserted business sector. Creek, who had been on duty, had the foresight to clear away the mess before anyone noticed.

Frisk does not see himself as a bad security man. He sees himself as doing what security staff have done since their inception: he is there as a deterrent, maintaining the illusion of security.

The rest of his time is devoted to the serious business of drinking.

Every evening, Frisk cycles five miles to an inexpensive corner shop, where he purchases his meagre food and whatever alcohol happens to be on offer that day, before cycling the five miles back to the empty building. This constitutes his exercise for the night, and he entertains the thought that its positive benefits will counteract the damage he is doing to his internal organs.

Aside from the small conversations with his family, or Creek, or the shopkeeper, or the man who calls round weekly to pay his wages, Frisk spends his time alone, drinking and listening to the radio.

The only radio station he's able to receive comes from overseas, in a language he doesn't understand, aside from the occasional English word or phrase amidst the babble. Often he can pick up an impression of what the DJs are saying, judging by the speakers' tone of voice, and by small, recurrent phrases that stand out to him as significant. The radio plays bland pop music, which Frisk mainly dislikes, yet as a replacement for the silence, he also finds it comforting.

As he sits, night after night, watching the green nightvision images of rows of desks lined with obsolete computer terminals, Frisk has the strangest thoughts. He invents stories about different worlds, alien societies, alternative realities. Occasionally, he feels that he ought to write some of these ideas down on paper, but is always stopped by the fear that nobody apart from him will ever read them; a thought that depresses him so much he has to drink even more than usual.

On the whole, Frisk is optimistic. He's spent hours reading through the training packs and confidential documents left behind by his former employers, and now considers himself to be as well read in the inner workings of the insurance industry as any company director. Come the economic upturn, he'll no doubt have a fine career ahead of him. In the meantime, he can relax and enjoy himself. Although at times he feels ancient, Frisk is still young, and will still be young when the happier times arrive.

Over the last few nights, he's been setting himself memory tests to strengthen his knowledge of insurance.

He sits, feet up on the desk, with a sandwich and a can of cider, nodding his head to the untranslatable tunes, running through the revision notes in his head.

He turns on the computer, and enters his user name and password.

The usual welcome screen greets him. Only tonight, there is something different:

You have one new message.

Frisk stops. He turns off the radio and absorbs the silence.

This building no longer has any web access, just the business intranet, which he and Creek never need to use. Yet, here is a message, presumably sent from one of the other computers in the building.

For a few moments, he is afraid to open it.

He goes for another walk, through the neighbouring office and around the reception area, preparing himself for the worst.

He returns to his desk. He swigs at the can of cider until it is empty.

He moves on to a second, finishing it in personal-best time.

He reaches forward and clicks.

Hello, reads the message.

My name is Clark Simper. I am an employee of Signa6ture Insurance Services, or I used to be, but am now trappped here on the 8th floor of their building, and have been since the business collapsedd.

I don't know if there is anyone in the company or in the building left to read this message, but if there is, please will you help me???///

As I think I have alr5eady said, I am trapped here on the 8th flooor. I am sorry if I am repeating myself, but I guess I am in the final stages of starvation, and probably don't make much sense, even to myself. I cannott even see these words that I am writing, as I am now more or less completely blind. I am able to touch-type, but not very well, as you can probably telll!!!

This is my last attempt at reaching out to the outside world. For the last 12 months, this room has not had a working phone line, or an electricity supply. The doors have, of course, been lockedd, and I have been unable to break through them, in spite of many att6empts.

9The fact that I have been completely unable to break my way out of the doors is a testament to how much this company once valued its security. As an employee I do, of course, respect that, but p0erhaps they should have paid a little more attentionn to matters of health and safety!!!!!!0

It also took me many atttempts to break into the vending machines, which have been my main source of food. There is a kitchen attached to this office, where staff used to make themselves snacks, and a defrosted fr5idge that has been sitting empty since I finished the last of the long-life milk. My hope almost ran out when I could no longer get water from the taps, or toilets. Over the last few w3eeks, I have been rationing myself with water from the large bottles used to refill the water cooolers. This supply is almost out too, after which I will only have my own urine, which I have already been drinking on a daily basis since the cutting off of the water supplyy.

I apologise for mentioning this, as I do not wish to upset anyone out there who may be reading this messsege. To be honest, it does not taste as bad as you may imagine. It is the temperature that I don't like - like a cup of tea that's been left a little too long. The trouble is, you have to drink it straight aw3ay to avoid it becoming infested with bacteria.

Anyway, my hope was almost gone until this morning, when by some act of an unknown god, the power supply started to work again. I was stilll unable to open the doors, but I was at least able to write this message. As I think I have said, this is my last attempt at contacting anybody, as all my other options have been used up. I have tried shouting until my throat is sore, but nobody seems to respond. A few weeks ago, I managed to break one of the windows by hurling a chair through it. The chair was not particullarly hefty, and the window was very strong, so it took several attempts, and lots of preciuus energy.

I imagined that if I did this, I would be able to draw attention to myself. I knew that I would not be able to climb down the wall, or jump. This is the eighth floor, and suicide is not in my nature.

My grandfather t6aught me to be a survivor. But that is a story for another time.

As I have already said, please help if you can, and if it is not too late. If there is anybody here to helpp.

Yours hopefully,
Clark Simper,
Accounts.

Frisk lets out a slow sigh of relief. A smile gratefully reaches his lips.

"Creek," he says aloud, "you are a sick man. That is just *not funny!*"

He breaks out into laughter, more out of relief than out of appreciation for the joke. He'd thought the message was genuine, until he saw the part about the chair, and knew this had to be Creek's doing. The message isn't exactly hilarious, but he laughs like he hasn't laughed in months, his chest rattling, his lungs gasping for air.

Here is something to tell his wife next time he calls. He knows that it's over with her, but at least they can still be friends.

He'll get Creek back tomorrow by telling him he went up to the eighth floor and got attacked by one of the squatters. Maybe he'll get some ketchup to rub on his face and pretend it's blood.

Still giggling, Frisk pulls out his sleeping bag from under the desk and curls up on the floor.

Nothing like having a good night's kip and getting paid for it.

◘

Meanwhile, eight floors above him, Clark Simper also lies on the carpet, clutching a piece of office stationery as though it's a good luck charm.

He closes his eyes.

He remains hopeful.

THE DAY SHE MELTED

The day she melted, she was shouting about how she's told me a thousand times, and I was shouting back telling her not to shout, when I noticed the dribbles of liquid flesh pouring down her face. She was in such a rage that she barely even noticed, and it wasn't long before she became just a puddle at my feet, leaving me no choice but to weep giant Alice tears until I melted too, mixing with her into one sweet swirling mass. We ran down the stairs, out the front door and down the street, waving at passers by as we rushed towards the bottom of the hill with no idea where we were going from here, but at least we were free.

VOOM AND BLOOM

To whom it may concern:
  I'm Voom, and I'm a liquid.
  I'm currently floating along a river in Europe.
  I can swim, without mixing in with the water. If I want to, I can climb out and run somewhere else.
  I run. That's what I do, see, because I'm a liquid.
  If you spill me out on to your table, I'll form a neat round puddle, no bigger or thicker than your dinner plate. But try to manipulate me in any way and you'll soon discover I'm not that sort of substance. I cannot be split into separate puddles, by even the most powerful tools. I cannot be frozen. I cannot be heated up and boiled and turned into a gas. At a million degrees, I don't even break a sweat. Whatever my conditions, I remain me. Only one. Almost.

I'm having a conversation with Bloom right now. Bloom is another liquid, living at present on a Pacific island at the top of a tree. Bloom likes birdwatching. She's telling me about all the different types of bird she's watched this week and all the strange names she's invented for them like "Pat" and "Steve", but I'm really not interested.
  Bloom's a freak.

As I swim, I have a memory of being a dolphin, with eyes, a tail and a brain. Solid, surrounded by expanses of liquid, and with more liquid on the inside.
  I remember being happy.
  I believe this is an artificial memory, implanted by a creature with a brain and some level of psychic ability—possibly a dolphin.
  It's not possible for me to have been a mammal in a former life.

I am a liquid. I am not alive. I was not born. I will not die.

I have memories of the future—of running into cracks in the ground, exploring the planet's core, bursting out through the top of volcanoes and geysers.

I'm looking forward to that.

My favourite past memory is of running into a microscopic stream and working my way into the body of a human—extending myself through his internal organs, clambering in and out of his network of veins and capillaries until I could see with his eyes, smell with his nostrils, taste his food, feel his sensations of love making.

I enjoyed being a human, but that was a phase. I got bored after a couple of decades.

◘

My least favourite past memory is of running into a sewer which I couldn't work my way out of for five days. I won't give you details.

My least favourite future memory is the quiet after the sun explodes.

Bloom's saying how she wants to meet up properly with me so we can be real friends, not just distant communicators. I'm reluctant, because I don't have a future memory of meeting Bloom, and anyway, I know what Bloom really wants. She wants to mix with me to combine ourselves into a new kind of liquid—stronger, more potent. A liquid that will take over the universe.

Why would I want to do that?

I'm Voom, thank you very much.

Voom Voom.

I climb out of the river and slither between blades of long grass. Bloom is going on about something to do with birds in the background (*freak*) but I'm not listening.

I'm thinking about what animal I'd like to be next. Maybe a dolphin again. Or a shark, or giraffe, or oak tree, or woodlouse.

Now I'm stopping as I catch something Bloom is saying on the other side of the world and realise what's been staring me in the face all this time.

I want to defy gravity. I want to have wings.

I have a new project, a fresh sense of purpose. Already I can see what the sea looks like from above in a newly formed future memory.

I make my way half a mile across the grass to the cluster of trees.

I climb one, almost to the top; locate a bird's nest, slink inside. Wait.

Bloom. The genius. In all this time I've never thought

But of course

I

No.

I've done this before.

I've had these feelings before.

I've been a bird before.

I've forgotten about it before.

Over and over.

I'm doing the same thing over and over again.

And now I'm panicking, because this is what happens when you've only got a rudimentary consciousness, and as with every attack of this kind, I am unable to handle the situation and fall asleep.

I'm having a dream about being a human. My name is Steve, and I live in Birmingham, England. I work for the Royal Mail. I don't have many friends, or a girlfriend, or a family around me, because my family is in Belfast. I moved over from Belfast for the change, and the work. I enjoy my work. I get up very early to go to the depot and sort the mail for delivery. I take my time with it, as I haven't yet got used to where all the streets are, and still carry a map. The blokes who work on my line have all been doing it for years, and hardly even need to look as they toss their letters and parcels at lightening speed into their allocated wooden slots. I enjoy this time, being part of a group of people, and we chat about the football. I avoid politics, even when they're discussing something trivial, like the buses or the foreigners. The rest of my working day is made up of pushing a bike with a sack of mail in and out of still-unfamiliar streets in all weathers. Usually it stays fine, which surprises me, as people complain about the rain all the time, yet it happens so rarely. In the evenings, I sit in my rented flat and watch TV, maybe phone home to see how they're doing, see if they fancy coming over to see me, or look for a place themselves. Sometimes I'll go out for a pint with a few of the boys from work, but I've not yet got the money to go out too often, and what with having to get up early in the morning, I don't like staying out late. We have a laugh. We watch the football, and the passing girls. Sometimes people ask me in hushed tones about the troubles, but there's nothing I can say. I just make a joke of it. "Postman Pat" they call me, because I'm Irish, even though I'm called Steve, and I haven't got anyone in my family called Patrick, or any friends called Patrick. I'm called Steve.

I'm awake again, waiting for the bird to arrive, thinking about how maybe I've got Bloom all wrong.

I try to speak to her, but she's asleep.

Maybe when the bird comes it will fly to the Pacific, and Bloom can watch, and I can call, "Look! It's me, Voom, I'm in the bird!"

It's peaceful up here.

SOME FACTS ABOUT ME

1. I'm a man.

2. I was one of ten children.

3. I spent twelve months of my life training to be a dentist.

4. For two years of my childhood, I insisted that I'd been abducted by aliens. The story was completely made up, and yet the more people reminded me of this fact, the more I insisted otherwise. It started as an innocent game, which developed into something more serious. It was probably a cry for attention directed at my inattentive parents. There were, inevitably, some children who believed my elaborate tales, and would ask me many questions, such as, "Did they perform experiments?" and "What did the aliens smell like?" It was as a result of these self-indulgent Q and A sessions that my lies were eventually exposed by the cross-examinations of an older cousin.

5. My name is Mark Greensleeves, and I am a liar.

The wonderful thing about that statement is that you have no way of telling whether it's true or not. If I am, indeed, a liar, why should you believe what I say? But if I'm telling the truth, it's a straightforward paradox.

There's a reason why liars don't form support groups.

6. I hate talking on the telephone. For one thing, I hate not being able to see the person that I'm speaking to.

You may think it's easier to lie over the phone, as the person you are talking to can't see your look of doubt. That's not a problem for me. Deception is only easier over the phone if you're not doing it properly.

But that isn't the reason I hate the telephone. I often like to entertain the idea that the universe was created just for me and my own entertainment. Other people and other objects are just an illusion, and when they are not standing in the same room as me, they are no longer there.

Some people say technology is responsible for urban isolation and the destruction of communities. If only that were true. The fact of the matter is, as soon as you're connected to a phone line, you're a click away from every single person in the industrialised world.

So much for privacy.

7. When I was a child, I was watching *Star Wars* with my older cousin, when Han Solo used the catchphrase, "May The Force Be With You," in a mocking tone.

"Is that man a goodie or a baddie?" I said.

"He's more of a goodie-baddie," said my cousin.

It's been one of my favourite expressions ever since. My favourite characters from fiction are always the goodie-baddies. They're always so much more complex and interesting than the standard figures of sympathy. Hamlet. 007. Judas.

8. I have no religious beliefs, but I find the idea of belief very interesting.

There is a man who stands on the corner of a street near my flat on Sunday afternoons preaching at the passers by that they are sinners who are yet to be saved. (Quite a judgmental attitude for a Christian, but I'll let that slide.)

I once approached the preacher, and asked him, "How can you believe in something you can't see?"

"Other people have seen, and written it down," he said.

"Someone sat down and wrote the *Mr Men* books," I said, "but it doesn't make them Gospel."

"I can't explain it to someone who doesn't have faith. It's something that I feel. I've never seen God, but I've felt Him."

"How do you know that what you felt was "God"? How do you know it wasn't just a part of yourself? In that case, you'd just be lying to yourself, wouldn't you?"

"If I'm lying to myself, then so be it. I'm happy with it."

"Doesn't God say that it's wrong to lie?"
I walked away, laughing.

9. And then there's disbelief. What is it that causes people to disbelieve something that can't be proven either way?

Suspension of disbelief is the process by which a person will listen to something they know not to be true, and yet disregard its falseness in order to feel sympathy for fictional characters, and process the emotional impact of imagined events.

Some suggest suspension of disbelief works because even though the fictions we are witnessing are indeed artificial, they also contain fundamental human truths.

I think there's more to it than that. In my view, the best fiction writers are the ones who push back the boundaries of believability, and allow us, for a short amount of time at least, to believe the unbelievable.

10. When I was seven years old, I was abducted by aliens.

It happened in my back yard one afternoon in June, when no one was around.

The aliens were very civil towards me. They took me into their space ship, which was invisible from the exterior, but once inside I was met by a lavish array of furnishings.

The aliens were purple, and smelt of vinegar.

They performed experiments on me, but only after receiving my consent. I was assured throughout the whole process that no harm would come to me, either physically or psychologically.

They also offered to erase my memory of the event, which I declined, only after some consideration.

In years to come, with hours spent trying to convince friends and relatives of what had happened, I would often regret not taking the other option. Things would have been easier that way.

11. My falsehoods are all my own work. I don't steal other people's ideas and pass them off as my own. Many people carry out this practise, and don't even regard it as deception.

My father had a favourite *Mail on Sunday* columnist who he used to plagiarise at length once a week around the crowded dinner table. The one thing my family agreed on was the quality of my mother's roast dinners, and therefore, on these occasions we were all too engrossed in our meals to be deterred by the old man's reactionary drivel.

Later, when he wasn't looking, I would dig the paper out from its perch and examine how accurately his distillation of the opinion piece had been. Often, certain words and phrases were underlined or circled. Once, he even managed to recite the whole thing verbatim.

There is nothing worse than a bad liar.

12. I hate being lied to. I can't stand it, especially when it's a lie that I've fallen for.

Some people might call me a hypocrite.

13. I can't stand it when someone doesn't believe me, especially when I'm lying. I'm sure that all the great actors are plagued by similar irritations.

Some people might call that self-doubt.

Luckily, for most of the time, I believe in myself, and I would like to think that others do too, at least for most of the time.

14. Sometimes, I like to pretend that my parents had ten children, but in actual fact, they only had three. We lived with seven of our cousins, who my parents also looked after, following an accident that killed my aunt. I was too young to remember them coming to live with us, and to be honest, there are very few things that I do remember about growing up. Sometimes stories that I've used to mythologize my childhood resurface in my mind as actual memories. It makes me wonder what are memories anyway, but thoughts in a person's head distorted by time and embellishment?

Perhaps if you tell a story enough times, it will become the truth.

15. There is one memory that returns to me with alarming regularity:

Lying in bed with Charlie. The setting sun was visible through the crack in the curtains, or so I imagine in hindsight.

"What are you thinking about?" she said.

What I was actually doing was perfecting some of the details of a story I was working on about myself. I was going to start telling people I spent twelve months training to be a dentist.

I couldn't tell her the story yet. I hadn't quite worked it all out.

Still, there's something about nakedness that goes hand in hand with honesty. It demonstrates that you have nothing to hide, and will share your thoughts as happily as you've shared your body. You'll never meet a dishonest naturist.

So instead, I said, "What?"

"What are you thinking about?"

"Nothing."

16. My cousin once told us a riddle about two brothers guarding the gates to Heaven and Hell. It is not clear which gate is which. One brother can only tell the truth, and the other can only tell lies. The riddle was this: if you only had one question to ask one of the brothers in order to ensure that you passed through the gates of Heaven, what would the question be?

"I know, I know!" I shouted out.

"Be quiet then," said my cousin. "Don't spoil it. Let the others guess."

I was lying. I had no idea what the answer was, and although my cousin told me, I can no longer remember it.

Sorry.

17. Deep down, I am passionate in my opposition to animal cruelty and intensive farming methods. I am not a vegetarian.

I am equally passionate in my opposition to the agents of climate change. I'll happily fly short-haul, and don't recycle.

I am strongly opposed to the treatment of workers in developing countries who are exploited by the wealthy, first world corporations who employ them. I have never boycotted any of their products, or criticised anyone else for doing the same.

This does not mean I'm apathetic about any of these issues. I am simply aware of the fact that one man's living habits will make absolutely no difference to the wider world.

I'm not being pessimistic. This isn't just my opinion. It's a fact, and if you give me a pen and paper I'll prove it. It's simple mathematics.

In order to make a difference, you need to get together with large groups of people who feel the same way as you.

Unfortunately, I don't like groups.

I don't fit into groups.

Groups and me don't mix.

It's hard enough dealing with people on a one to one basis.

18. Charlie was my longest relationship. She lasted three months. During that time, I was happier than I have ever been.

I also told more lies during those three months than I'd probably told in the previous three years.

I invented an entire life for myself. I was an only child. I was exceptionally gifted academically, which meant that I had to be moved two years ahead in school, partly for my own benefit, but it was also felt that my intelligence was putting the other children off. I excelled even in these higher years, which again did not win me any friends, so my parents took me out of education altogether in order to teach me at home. My father was a noted science professor and environmental campaigner who turned down a research post at Oxford in order to dedicate his time to me. I would have liked to have said that he taught me everything I knew, but this would be misleading. My father taught me how to learn, which is something I never received at school.

When he died, me and my mother were by his side. His final words to me were: "I hope that when it is you who is lying here, and your loving wife and son are sitting by your side, you will have been able to say that you've had as few regrets as I've had."

There were many other stories, too numerous to mention here. Many of them were based on existing lies I'd told a thousand times before, but in order for them all to fit together I had to construct a thousand other lies to fill in the gaps. The whole process was exhausting. When it finished, I imagined that I missed Charlie, but really I missed the part I was playing. This was particularly tragic for me, because I knew that I could never play that role again, not properly anyway. The role you play has to suit the audience you're playing it to. I tailor-made every detail to match Charlie's idea of what her perfect partner should be. Or, at least, that was my perception of it.

In the end, I was caught out by a simple lie. A basic mistake that I couldn't simply invent a new story to cover up for.

She found out my real name.

19. My Mum forgot my name once.

I've heard people talk about this phenomenon in affectionate terms before. Your mother will accidentally call you by the name of one of your siblings and then correct herself. Sometimes she'll go through a whole list of names before she gets to yours. That's not what happened with me. My Mum *actually forgot my name.*

It happened when I was a teenager. She was driving me to the cash and carry because she wanted me to lift some boxes.

"Fasten your seatbelt, er..." she said.

"Fasten your seatbelt *what?*" I said.

My Mum put her fingers to her lips. "Fasten your seatbelt *please?*" she said.

I looked at her, testily. "What's my name?"

My Mum gave a nervous giggle. "What kind of question is that?"

"I'm not fastening my seatbelt until you tell me my name," I said.

My Mum shifted in her seat, seemingly not sure whether to tell me off for answering back or admit defeat.

"It's on the tip of my tongue," she said.

I fastened my seatbelt. "Forget about it," I said.

"You're not going to remind me?" she said.

"It's not important," I said.

We drove to the cash and carry in silence. My Mum turned up the radio in a bid to ease the tension.

Six weeks later, we were eating Sunday dinner. My Dad was in the middle of one of his lectures.

"Could you pass the gravy, Mark?" my Mum whispered to me.

I didn't say anything. I just passed her the gravy.

People say that I make some of these stories up about my childhood, and they're right, I do. But I didn't make this one up. Believe it or not, this really happened.

20. When I was eight years old, I was suspended from school for continually insisting that I'd been abducted by aliens. The suspension came about as a result of a heated argument between myself and my class teacher. While my teacher repeatedly ordered me not to "tell tales," I insisted that it was my duty to impart knowledge that happened to be true – an obligation shared by the institution we belonged to.

My parents were advised to send me to a child psychologist – an offer they declined on the grounds that I was only doing it for attention. At the time, I respected their decision. They must have known what they were talking about, because they were grownups.

Now that I'm a grownup myself, I would still be inclined to agree with them.

After all, it's not as though I was making the story up.

21. In certain selected circles, I used to pretend that I spent school breaktimes selling my stash of duty-free cigarettes to fellow pupils, in exchange for answers to homework questions, or favours such as getting an enemy beaten up. In this scenario, I went to an inner-city comprehensive, and my parents were unemployed. Nonetheless, they were the best parents I could ever have wished

for, and it was only their tireless perseverance that kept me from pursuing a life of crime.

22. In other circles, I've painted myself as having been a great athlete, who would sweep the board at sports days, and was in the Chelsea under-14s. I could've gone professional later in life if I hadn't jumped in front of a speeding truck to save a young girl's life. I broke both my legs and arms, but to this day, I've maintained that the injuries were worth it. The girl was fine, and went on to play a long-standing role in the television soap opera, *Coronation Street*.

In this version of events, I was a middle class grammar school boy. Although my parents had money, I was never spoiled, and I was always taught to care for those less well off than myself.

23. The truth is, my school life was largely unremarkable. I had a handful of friends, and we kept out of trouble. We were neither a cause for concern, nor a shining example. We were just normal people trying to get through the difficult years without undergoing the embarrassment of standing out.

At breaktimes we used to hang out in the library. This was not due to any of us being academically gifted. It was just a place to go.

One lunchtime, a group of us were sitting round a table, playing coin football, just passing the time.

My friend Luke turned to me and said, "Did you know, the word gullible isn't in the dictionary?"

"Why isn't it?" I said.

"It just isn't. It's just a fact that I know."

"Really?"

"Look it up if you don't believe me."

I went over to the shelves and pulled down the biggest dictionary I could find.

"You liar," I said, "it's right here!"

I turned around to show them, only to be met by a chorus of chuckling faces.

"Yeah, why don't you read what it says?" said Luke. "It's you: Mark-Greenie-Greensleeves."

That was the last time I ever fell for a joke like that. Now I'm constantly on my guard. Every day is April 1st as far as I'm concerned.

24. The last time I spoke to Charlie was on the telephone.

"Why?" she was saying to me. "Why didn't you just tell me? What's so shameful about your real name that you can't share it?"

"There's nothing shameful about it. I just call myself Mark Greensleeves. I prefer it."

"Is that what your parents called you?"

"No."

"Is that what people called you at school?"

"No."

"So why did you tell me that story?"

"What story?"

"You don't even remember. You told me kids in the playground used to tease you about your name. They called you "Greenie," and "Snotty," and "The Bogeyman". I felt sorry for you. Is that what you wanted?"

"I know it was wrong. But it's such a small thing. Such a little lie. What does it matter what my real name is? I never meant to hurt you."

"Well, you have, Mark. Or whatever your name is."

"I've never told a malicious lie in my life. I may tell the odd white one for my own amusement, or to make myself look a bit more interesting. But I would never deliberately hurt anyone."

"I don't believe you."

"You have to believe me."

"I can never believe anything you tell me again."

"But I'm actually telling the truth."

"Could you promise me you'll never lie to me again?"

"Honestly? No, I can't promise that. I can promise that I'll never intentionally hurt you by lying."

"That's stupid."

"I know it is. This is the person that I am. But you have to understand that I'm not bad."

"I don't think you're bad, Mark. I just can't do this anymore."

"Look," I said, "all I wanted – all I've ever wanted ..."

"Have a good life, Mark."

"Look, just *listen* to me. All I've ever wanted is for someone to *listen* to me. Just listen to what I have to say. You don't have to believe me, and you don't have to love me. I just want you to *listen* ..."

The line went dead.

25. If I could offer one piece of advice to anyone thinking of taking up lying seriously, it is this: if you want to be a good liar, it's necessary for you to believe the lie yourself. As long as you believe the lie yourself, then no matter how bizarre or outlandish it happens to be, other people will believe it too. Not everyone will believe it, of course. People have their own minds, and you are not a miracle worker.

Some people don't believe the truth either. Some people are idiots.

For a lie to work for me, it has to contain some element of truth. It wouldn't work otherwise, because I wouldn't believe it myself.

That day in June when I was seven, I was standing in the back yard on my own, when a low-flying aircraft passed overhead. It was only a small plane, but to a small child it might as well have been a jumbo jet, and it was flying so low, I almost thought it was going to crash into the house.

I ducked my head.

When I dared to look up again, the plane was already heading into the distance.

As I stood there, slightly shaken by the experience, I began to consider what might have happened if the plane had been flying lower.

As I stood there some more, I imagined what would have happened if the plane wasn't a plane at all.

There was no one there to say that it was a plane, or it wasn't a plane.

There was just me, standing on my own, and when you're standing on your own, anything is possible.

That may have been the greatest moment of my life. No other people to tell me I was wrong. Just me, and a world of possibility.

I can't remember all the details now, but whenever I picture it, the sun is shining, and there are no clouds, just the faintest streak of white that slowly fades as I make my plans.

It's a beautiful day.

THE OPENING

I was new in town.

I'd quit the previous town pretty quickly for a number of pressing reasons, all of which were serious and none of which were my fault.

I needed cash badly, so I booked into the first B&B I could find and headed straight for the job centre.

I found an advertisement with a number to ring, and the contact name of a Mr N. Fitzpatrick.

"O-PEN!" greeted the voice on the line. "Nathan Fitzpatrick speaking!"

Now, I've worked with some fairly unpleasant characters in the past, and to be honest, I was expecting more of the same.

Fitzpatrick, however, was a genuine inspiration. Before I could even introduce myself, he was insisting that I call him Nathan, and recounted the history of his business as though I were the first person in the world to hear it.

He told me of his humble beginnings setting up a stall in a market, selling the first ever O-PEN products: various novelty items that doubled up as pens. He referred to everything by its full name —"Key Fob That Is Also A Pen"; "Harmonica That Is Also A Pen" — never abbreviating, or growing tired of the repetition.

Nathan's vision stretched far beyond his initial setting. His dream was for every household to be stocked with appliances that were also pens, with at least one in each room, so that no matter where you were in the house you would not be left short in a crisis.

Unfortunately, in those early days, his pens were simply not being taken seriously. They continued to be regarded as mere gimmickry, by both his competitors and an increasingly patronising general public.

And so, in an attempt to assert himself, Nathan had now ditched any item that was not regarded as a household necessity. His greatest triumph thus far was the product I'd now be selling: "The Vacuum Cleaner That Is Also A Pen".

Very interesting stuff, of course.

The problem was, I was calling from the phone box on the high street, and as there was no logical point in which to interrupt his narrative (a tale far more complex than the version I choose to recount here) I had no option but to stand there and listen, watching my money gradually vanish, every so often reaching up and dropping in another pound.

Money was so tight at that time that I was carefully regulating all of my outgoings. Strictly, the coins I'd wasted on the phone call were meant for that afternoon's lunch. Although I needed the job from Nathan, I was so annoyed by him effectively stealing my lunch money that I called him a playground bully and demanded compensation.

"Don't worry about it," he said. "In fact, allow me to take you to lunch."

He explained more about the job over a cheeseburger and fries.

I was to be given my own car and phone, all expenses paid.

"I'll be honest with you, Nath." I said, "I like the way you do business."

"Well, thank you," he said. "The job is yours. But then, I don't suppose I really needed to say that." He looked deep into my eyes. "You know that already. This job has always been yours. It is your calling."

For a moment, I was suspicious. "You're not religious, are you?" I said.

"Yes," he said. "My religion is Vacuum Cleaners That Are Also Pens."

"Nathan Fitzpatrick," I said, "you are a welcome shaft of light in a dark and hopeless world."

My hand went up to scratch my nose. I hoped he didn't notice.

The following morning, I was on the road in my car with my phone in its holder and a pocket full of personalised business cards that

Nathan had produced.

I arrived at my first house: Ms M. Hex.

The woman who opened the door seemed a little dubious at first, but within minutes we were demonstrating the vac's awesome power on her carpet. Not having seen these machines in action before, I was pleasantly surprised.

I stood back, arms folded.

"You know, it doesn't matter how many times I see these little babies in action, I cannot help but be impressed by them."

I turned off the machine.

"Do you have any questions, Ms Hex?"

"Yes," she said, her arms also folded. "Why the pen?"

"Obvious reasons, really," I said. "So that you can have something to write with."

I demonstrated. The pen was attached to its own flexible plastic tube, which extended itself from the top of the machine and could stretch as far as three metres in any direction.

"You see? There's no chance of losing *this* behind the sofa, Ms Hex."

"Well, OK," she said, "but if I wanted to keep hold of a pen that badly, I'd get one of those pens on chains from the bank. I'm impressed by your Hoover, but to be honest, you seem like a bit of a crackpot."

I improvised. "I *am* a crackpot! Wahey!" I performed a cartwheel in the middle of the carpet. "But I'm crackers *about this product*, Ms Hex. Pens at the bank, you say? I think we both know where such items belong. What kind of a homely feel are you going to get from pens on chains? Free the pens, I say. Free the pens! And treat them with respect. Ours is a disposable culture, Ms Hex. We use a pen, the ink runs out, we throw it away and buy another one. Or else we lose the pen behind the sofa, letting it sit there for months, lidless; the ink dries out, you find it, funnily enough, while you're doing the vacuuming; you throw it away. Or else you keep it, not realising it no longer works. You keep it until a very important piece of information transpires that you need to write down. You pick up the pen—it doesn't work. You scribble furiously—nothing.

You forget what it was you had to write down and you throw the pen away in anger and bitter frustration. *Or*—you may not notice the pen sitting there behind the sofa. It may be sucked up into the vacuum cleaner, breaking it—your brand-new vacuum cleaner that you bought at the recommended retail price without discount, with a guarantee that does not extend to "pen damage". Again, the frustration, the anger. The answer? Attach the pen to the vacuum cleaner!

"Now, the beauty of this product, Ms Hex, is that not only is it two products in one, but both of these products are the leaders in their respective fields. The vacuum cleaner—well, we've seen what that can do. The pen? Observe."

I reached down and wrote my fake name, *Preston North End*, on a scrap of paper and handed it to her.

"With these pens, there is no need to scribble. It will remain at this quality for the rest of its existence. When the ink runs out, you simply refill it."

"And I suppose I have to pay for all the refills?" said Ms Hex.

"Of course you don't," I said. "All refills are provided by O-PEN completely free of charge."

Ms Hex was so impressed by this that she did not respond when both of my hands reached up to scratch my nose.

"And the money?" she said.

"OK," I said. "Now, seeing as you've been so inquisitive, I'd like to reward you with a neat little discount. These machines generally retail at around £400. I can quote you today £375."

"Seems a bit steep," she said.

"I'm going to be honest with you, Ms Hex: this is an expensive product. There are valid reasons why it is expensive. The quality you have seen today speaks for itself. You used the word 'Hoover' earlier. Never use that word again. From now on, there are no Hoovers; there are not even any vacuum cleaners. There are only O-PEN vacuum cleaners."

"OK," she said.

I gave her my card and told her to contact me if she ran into any trouble with the equipment. I assumed it would be some time before she realised that the card did not include an address or phone number, just the initials P.N.E. and O-PEN in attractive lettering.

From then on, it was easy. I was making twenty-five percent on each sale, which meant £95.75 for what averaged out at thirty minutes' work, if you didn't include the drive. This meant £500 to £600 on a good day.

Soon I had enough money to find a good place to live, but decided to stay at the B&B for a while longer. I was dedicating so much time to selling that any time spent otherwise was considered a waste. I ate a full English every morning, and found that this filled me up enough to work through lunch. In the evenings, I would eat take-away and watch TV, paying close attention to the adverts.

My nose developed a rash. It began as one spot right in the middle, which appeared the morning after my first sale. Whenever I saw Nathan, he'd call me Rudolph and slap me on the back a little too hard for my liking. One spot soon became a cluster of spots and it was becoming impossible for me to leave them alone. I tried all sorts of creams and ointments, but they seemed to irritate the skin still further. The rash soon spread to the inside of my nostrils, and any public scratching—which had proved inevitable at times—made me appear to be picking my nose.

Still, I was making so much money it was quite unthinkable for me to take time out to see a doctor. Instead, I prescribed for myself a strict regime of painkillers and controlled scratching. Every hour, on the hour, I allowed myself five minutes' scratching time. All other scratching was forbidden, and aside from a few isolated incidents that were quite beyond my control, I stuck to the system. If I happened to be at a customer's house, as was often the case, and the time would reach the o'clock, I would politely ask if I might use their bathroom. One time I was refused this privilege and, unable to resist, I began scratching like a madman for five full minutes, only explaining after I had done so, "I have a rash, you see

..."

One morning when I arrived at Nathan's office to collect more vacuum cleaners I decided to take the opportunity to share a few of my ideas with him. Nathan was seldom around by this stage, sometimes going missing for weeks at a time, and the new management he'd brought in never seemed to know what was going on, so I decided not to delay.

"I'd like to take a more active role in the company's output," I told him. "I know you're hoping to expand the range soon, Nath— but when? And with what?"

"Really none of your business," he said.

"I've got lots of ideas. 'Hair-Drier That's Also A Pen'; 'Washing Machine That's Also A Pen'; and how's about *this*: a grandfather clock! You put the pen in the pendulum. *Pen*dulum—you get me?"

"Word of advice, Rudolph," he said. "Perhaps you ought to concentrate on your actual *job* rather than expansion ideas."

I couldn't tell if he were joking or not. "What do you mean? I'm making *excellent* ..."

"No doubt you are, Rudolph—one vacuum cleaner at a time. Your problem is, you go in there expecting to sell one, and that's all you ever do! You need to be going in there expecting to sell ten, and if you come out having sold nine, well, that's still a disappointment. So you tell yourself you're definitely going to make ten sales next time, and lo and behold ...!"

"With respect, Nathan," I said, "it's not quite as simple as that."

"It's not *rocket science*, Rudolph. This product sells itself, you know that. And another thing: you're not following up enough leads. You know your problem? It's not that you spend too much time on an appointment, you don't—you just drive like an old woman!"

"So I like to drive carefully ..."

"Do you know how many sales Brian makes in a week?"

"No."

"Much more than you, and it's not because of multiple sales —he's just as diabolical as you are in that department. Brian makes more because he breaks the speed limit. Think about it. You know your problem?"

"I think you just told me."

"You're *happy*. You're happy to live in your little B&B with your little TV and your five sales a day. Expansion ideas? I've got news for you, Rudolph, something that may not have occurred to you, maybe you didn't pay attention in physics: if a pendulum stops swinging, *the clock stops*! Bye bye!"

I tried to look into his eyes, but they were directed at the desk as though I'd already left.

"What happened to you, Nathan? Your words of encouragement, your ... your sage wisdom?"

"Try not to trap your conk in the door on the way out," he said.

My nose got worse. The itching had died down to be replaced by an ache that started in the middle of my head and at times seemed to extend to the section of air two feet in front of my face.

I had decided to combat the skin irritation by not scratching at all. I attached a bandage. If I'd been to the doctor's, no doubt they would advise that I allow the skin to breathe, but I felt I was safer from harm that way. Several times I had scratched until I'd bled and continued regardless. To make doubly sure I did not scratch, I had superglued a pair of black leather gloves to my hands and attached small pieces of broken glass to the fingertips. I kept the glue remover in a locked box beneath the bed, promising myself not to open it until the rash was completely healed.

I missed a night of sleep due to the ache.

That morning was the first in weeks that I was unable to eat my breakfast. Instead I stared down at the plate and drank seven cups of coffee.

Usually, I would make polite conversation with fellow guests, occasionally making a sale after explaining what I did for a living, but that morning I remained silent. An old couple were taking it in turns to look over at me, but I couldn't be bothered explaining.

On my arrival at my first appointment, a Mr J. Switch, I'd pulled myself together somewhat.

The man opened the door to find me standing there with the vac at my feet and my hands behind my back, bunched into a pair of loose fists so as to disguise the broken glass.

"Mr Switch! *Top of the morning to you*, as I believe runs the popular Irish ..."

He looked almost as though he wasn't going to let me in.

"I think there's been some sort of communications breakdown," he said. "I dialled 1471 after receiving the call from your marketing people, but it came up number withheld. I tried the phone book, the Yellow Pages, Directory Enquiries, all the different ones. Eventually, I called the police."

"Mr Switch, why on earth would you do something like that?"

"Oh, I'm not saying you're *criminals,* or anything. I just wanted to get in touch to cancel the appointment. I don't need a new vacuum cleaner. I'm sorry."

"*Need,* Mr Switch? You'll be surprised. A few weeks ago, I sold one of these babies to my old friend Lord Briarston, and just to test it we set about cleaning one of the carpets at his private estate. Now, although the carpet had been supposedly 'cleaned' a thousand times before, our machine sucked up so much dust—dust other vacuum cleaners *simply cannot reach*—that Lord Briarston calculated that due to carpet's age some of that dust could have been sitting there for *generations*. Just to see, we ran some DNA tests, and sure enough found the dead skin cells of half of Lord Briarston's family tree. Not only that—there were heads of state in there as well! *Queen Victoria* was in there! Queen Victoria's DNA! Needless to say, we auctioned off the bag and made enough money to give the building a much-needed renovation. All thanks to O-

PEN." I patted the vacuum cleaner on the head.

"That's all very well," said Mr Switch. "But how are people supposed to *contact* you?"

"Well, initially, Mr Switch, we will contact you. Consider it a personal service. Now, I'm not going to lie to you: I am a salesman. I am here to try to sell you a Vacuum Cleaner That Is Also A Pen. You may not, as you say, 'need' a new vacuum cleaner. You may not, as you quite rightly suggest, feel that you 'need' a new pen. But how will you know if you don't give these products a chance?"

"Is there a website?" he said.

"A website, Mr Switch? A website? We are a family company!"

I took hold of the pen by slotting it into my closed hand and extended its attachment until it reached an inch away from my customer's face.

"Do you know what this represents? Family values. Tradition. You know where you *are* with a pen, Mr Switch. If I write something down on a piece of paper, it's *there*, it's in my hand, it's not virtual. There's no chance of it getting infected by a virus or accidentally being deleted, erased forever. If I lose a piece of paper behind the sofa, it's *still there*. Even if I burn it, it's *still there*, it's just been converted into scattered carbon molecules. You see?"

"I think you'd better come in," he said.

I entered his house.

I demonstrated the vacuum cleaner.

I demonstrated the pen.

Then certain things started to go wrong.

My nose started twitching. I reached up instinctively to stop it. My palm connected with my nose while my fingers made small incisions all over my face. I pulled my hand away and cursed my foolishness, and as I did so, I clenched my fist, piercing the leather and cutting my hand. Blood dribbled on to the carpet.

"Don't worry," I said. "That vacuum cleaner nozzle has an in-built stain remover that'll shift just about anything!"

As I was saying this, my nose continued twitching, and my resistance to touch it was so weak that I was hopping up and down on the spot.

Mr Switch was standing mesmerised as though all of this were too much information to take in.

Suddenly, he snapped out of his trance.

"I'd better take four," he said.

I was pleased, but still, sympathy sales did not come along very often and it was not enough to get me through the day.

I hadn't mentioned the discount yet, so I quoted him £1600 and he reached for his chequebook.

In a flash of inspiration, when he asked me who he could make the cheque out to, instead of giving my usual "O-PEN Limited", I told him my own name, my real name, and from there on, that money was mine, the car was mine, the phone was mine.

"Thank you," I said as I left, "and don't hesitate to contact me any hour of the day or night about those free refills."

I did not leave a business card.

I drove out of town, through the next town and through the next, wondering where I would decide to stop, or if I would ever stop driving again.

A mass of images flashed through my head, some good, some bad, each of them dictating my mood for the short time they remained.

For no good reason, Nathan Fitzpatrick's face popped into my head, and an almost unbearable rage overcame me.

If it wasn't for *him*, if it hadn't been for *him* ...

A fresh pain shot through my face, sharper than ever before, as though I were giving birth the wrong way up.

I pulled to the side of the road.

I closed my eyes for several minutes, not daring to look.

Finally, I opened them. I adjusted the driver's mirror to examine my blood-flecked image, with water in its eyes and a new addition protruding through its bandage.

My nose had grown a clear inch.

I examined my side-profile, imagining the kind of shadow I would cast, and found myself wincing. I could see it hanging there in front of me without needing to look down.

The pain had disappeared now. This in itself was a kind of

relief.

I removed the bandage.

The rash had also gone, just pinkish traces left in the skin.

The tears continued to flow, real emotional ones this time.

This wasn't my fault. That was the crying shame. None of this was my fault.

I reached for the phone, and from memory dialled the number of my surgeon from several towns previously.

"I need another reduction," I told him. "It's happened again."

"I'll book you in for tomorrow morning," he said. "Discretion assured as always, sir."

As I turned off the phone, I found myself remarking sardonically to myself that *this* was where all my money went.

I opened the phone from the back, took out the battery, removed the SIM card and threw it out of the window.

I twisted the keys, took off the handbrake, put my foot down, and performed a U-turn without signalling.

THE WONDERING

I'm walking home from work thinking about paper aircraft, and how some people can make really intricate ones that fly for miles, but when I was a kid I could only ever make those crap paper darts that nose-dive after the first few inches. I could get Janet to teach me, because she has all these really amazing talents like painting and making papier mâcher sculptures that she never finds time to develop because she's too busy with the flat, and her morning job, but I'm sure she'll be able to make a decent plane.

I'm at the crossing just across from my block.

I'm waiting, but the cars keep streaming past, and no one even notices me standing here. I'm too tired to wave or make a fuss.

It's getting late, though.

Janet will be up in the flat across the street, cooking my dinner and making sure the living room's tidy so I can watch my TV shows in a clutterless environment, because if I've told her once I've told her a thousand times, I can't stand dirt in my house.

She'll also be wondering where I am.

I used to have trouble relating to people, and understanding that sometimes they do things differently from me, including having different views, moods and preferences. That's why I came up with these mantras to say in my head whenever I get wound up by something small. I'd chant them over and over until they became almost part of my body, in tune with my heartbeat:

I love the world.

I want to share my love with the world.

If I share my love with the world, the world will love me back.

Repeat, repeat, repeat.

Now I'm looking at my watch, and I must've fallen into a trance, because I've been waiting for the traffic to part for eight hours.

It's three o'clock in the morning and the cars are still moving.

At some point Janet must've realised and come downstairs, or shouted out of the window, but once I'm in the zone, I don't even notice shouting.

I'm waving my arms at the motorists now and yelling "STOP, YOU FUCKERS!" but still they continue.

It's only now that I realise the drivers are all lobsters.

Big, red, fuck-off lobsters the size of humans, tapping at the pedals with their tails and twisting the steering wheels with surprisingly agile pincers.

It's not a big deal, it's just something that happens to me sometimes.

I was wondering how long it would take, actually. At least now the lobsters are back, it takes the wondering away. The wondering's the worst part.

I live in a block of flats, located in the middle of a concrete island. The lobsters are just driving round and round the block in their speeding circle of vehicles.

There's no way I'm gonna risk making a dash for it. These fuckers'll kill me instantly at the speed they're going, and probably won't even brake.

Janet will be in bed by now. I hope they don't wake her. It's not fair to get Janet involved.

I want to get some bricks from down an alley and come running back and scream and smash the windscreens, not to make them stop, just to piss them off, just to show them they haven't won. But where's the sense in that?

Let's look at the reality of the situation: I'm probably not going to be able to cross this road tonight. I can either throw bricks and shout and scream, or—and this is the voice of experience talking—I can just walk away.

So, that's what I do, and I'm proud of myself, because a couple of years ago, or maybe even a couple of months ago, I would've gone to get the bricks.

This is what I mean when I talk about *sharing the love*. Sometimes sharing the love can mean walking away and not hurting anyone, human or otherwise.

Beyond my block, the roads are empty, with queues of parked cars on either side.

I'd like to think that somewhere these things are happening to other people too. You never see this stuff on the news, but surely there's nothing strange or special about little old me.

I'm tired. I don't have the money for a hotel, so I walk to the park and fall asleep on a bench, chanting to myself under my breath: *If I share my love with the world, the world will love me back.*

It makes me feel a bit warmer.

Now I'm awake with the sun in my eyes, and I'm lying on the concrete path beside the bench where one of the lobsters has superglued me to the ground. The little fucker's up a tree, and he's woken me up by flicking acorns at my head.

Fine way to start the day.

Fucking lobsters.

The whole thing takes me back to childhood when I used to play in the park on the swings and fantasise about swinging all the way round and round again like a propeller and then just flying off somewhere, me and my swing.

Now I'm happy, lying on my back in a puddle of acorns, while further acorns tap against my forehead. I hardly even feel them now, because I know that no matter what the lobsters try to do to me, they are not going to win. If I don't retaliate, if I just lie here and ignore them, they'll eventually get bored and give up.

I don't remember the first time the lobsters started appearing, or how many times they've appeared to me now. It all just blends in together to form a long, rambling epic that's best forgotten anyway.

I just want to get a swimming pool full of boiling water and chuck them all in. Push them off the diving board and watch them bubble.

Janet's not that bad. She looks after me, and cooks my dinner, and always makes sure I'm wearing a clean shirt, even when she's angry with me. I always worry that one day she'll realise that all the trouble I get myself into isn't really worth it, but until that happens —*if*, I should say ...

The lobsters in the cars should be gone by now, and she'll be waking up, wondering when and if I'll be home.

When I get back, I know I won't be able to explain myself, and she'll question me, and keep on at me until I get angry and frustrated, the way that I always do when she does this, and I'll shout at her, and maybe throw something against the wall to show her who's boss—a plate, or something we can easily replace.

As long as I don't throw *her* against the wall like I did that one time. That was a mistake. There's no replacing Janet.

It'll be OK in a few days, after we've had chance to settle back into our routine.

I know she just says these things to test me. I know that she secretly knows about the lobsters, but I also know that I'd destroy her belief in them if I actually said it out loud. This is the way that we communicate—on a different level. I'm not saying it's the ideal way to do things, or that other people should try it. Sometimes, it's just a fucking nuisance.

But I don't see it as wrong. It's just the way we do things.

It's not wrong.

It's just *different*.

THE WORLD

May 24th:

Didn't go in to work this morning. Really not feeling myself.

I've lost my ability to judge distance. When I opened my eyes, everything from the alarm clock beside me, to the sun that shone through the gap in the curtains appeared before me as equal.

I lay in bed for a while, observing all the many objects floating before my face, without a clear indication of their place in the world.

I was unsure of how I was supposed to move.

I came to the conclusion that I would still be able to walk around the house, as I already knew where everything was, even if my perception of their positions had been altered.

The stairs were the worst part. I closed my eyes as I made my way down, with hands clutching onto the wall.

I sat on the sofa, finding myself able to see many things that I knew were not in the room with me. To offer some obvious examples, amongst the crowd of images, I could make out the Eiffel Tower, the Pyramids of Egypt and the Great Wall of China. But such landmarks are not in any way impressive when you have the whole planet sitting there in your range of vision. It was all tiny, but I could see it all clearly. Everything appeared to be the same distance away as everything else.

I raised my hand to my eyes and waved, but my fingers now appeared as though they were many miles away, like a sailor waving from a distant ship.

Somehow, I managed to eat some toast.

I think I'd better go back to bed.

May 25th:

I awoke expecting things to be different.

They are.

I can now see the world with much sharper definition. I can examine the patterns on the backs of fish in the furthest seas. I can analyse each individual grain of sand in the remotest desert.

I have also regained the ability to perceive distance. Objects appear bigger and smaller depending on their proximity. Today when I wave my hand before my eyes, it fills the entire room, and seems to cast a shadow over the world at my feet.

I made myself a bowl of cereal, but had to keep my eyes closed the whole time to avoid being dazzled.

I watched as every single human, animal and plant on the planet went about their daily routines.

All I've done today is sit here and watch. There is endless entertainment. Endless beauty.

When you can see everything, there's no such thing as day and night. There's both at the same time.

I didn't bother calling into work this morning.

The phone rang and I unplugged it.

I'm looking forward to dreaming tonight.

May 26th:

My friend Salvador came to visit this morning. I didn't want to let him in, but he kept knocking and ringing the bell.

I invited him in, and asked him to make me a drink.

I sat waiting in the living room, and he brought me through a cup of coffee.

"So, what's the matter with you?" he said. "Why haven't you been at work?"

"Nothing," I said, "nothing, really."

"Why have you got your eyes closed?" he said.

"Headache," I said.

"I'll close the curtains."

"That won't make a difference."

Salvador closed the curtains anyway.

"I'm really not good company at the moment," I said.

"I'm just concerned about you," said Salvador. "Has something happened?"

"Nothing's happened. Nothing really."

"Nothing "really"? So has something small happened? Sometimes a small thing can affect you in a big way."

"I don't know," I said.

"It might help to talk."

"I don't want to talk."

"I'm your friend," he said. "You can tell me anything, and I'll keep it a secret."

"I want you to leave now," I said. "I've got a headache, and I want to lie down."

"So, there is something, isn't there?"

"Maybe there is. I don't want to talk about it. If you're my friend, you should respect that."

"Will you tell me another day?"

"Maybe. We'll see."

"Can I get you anything from the chemist?"

"I'm not ill."

"For your head?"

"No thank you."

"I think I'd better go."

"OK."

"See you later in the week?"

"Maybe."

May 27ᵗʰ:

Today, sight is accompanied by sound. I can hear everything in the world. Every conversation, every piece of music; the crashing of every wave. But instead of coming across as an incoherent rabble, I can understand each individual sound, and differentiate one from another. I can choose to ignore the noises I don't like, and focus on those that I do. I listen to people talking, and can understand any word in every language.

I sit, watch and listen.

Time passes as though it were never there.

May 28th:

I haven't eaten for two days. I'm running out of food, and I know that if I step outside I'll be overwhelmed. These walls are a shield against the beauty of the world.

I phoned Salvador earlier, and told him I needed his help.

"What do you need?" he said.

"I need you to buy me some groceries. I'll give you the money."

"No problem," he says. "But first I need you to tell me what's bothering you."

"I can't tell you that," I said.

"Then I can't help you."

I knew I should've made up a story to satisfy him, but I found myself completely unable to lie.

"I can't tell you on the phone," I said. "Buy me the food and I'll tell you when you get here."

I watched as Salvador left his house, and bought the items I'd requested. I watched as he walked up to my door, and pushed the bell.

I'd disconnected it.

He knocked on the door, but I didn't reply.

He called me from his mobile, but I'd unplugged the phone again.

It took him a few moments to realise I'd left the money I owned him in an envelope on the doorstep.

He carried on knocking for another ten minutes, and shouted through the letterbox.

Eventually he went home, leaving the shopping at the door.

I had to close my eyes when I collected the bags.

Time to eat.

May 30th:

Something is different today. I can read people's minds. I hear their thoughts and see their dreams as they sleep.

My mind is full of stories. Many of these stories are the same, while others have their own unique twists and surprises.

It occurs to me that witnessing these events ought to provoke a whole range of emotions, but I don't seem to react to them in sympathy, even when they're extremely happy or sad. Everything pales in comparison to the experience of seeing and hearing and knowing everything there is to see, hear and know.

I ate a full meal today, and I can feel myself growing stronger.

Perhaps I could go for a walk, if I wore a pair of sunglasses.

Not today, though.

May 31st:

I did a bad thing today.

As I sat watching the world, I wondered if I could alter it in some way.

It's something I've been thinking about for some time now, wondering what I'd do if I was able to influence the way the world worked. For days, I've been plagued by the temptation to reach out and touch.

To put my theory to the test, I decided to choose a guinea pig; someone expendable. It would have to be a person I didn't like.

The name that sprang to mind almost instantly was Martin Jeffries.

I hadn't seen Martin Jeffries for years. At school, he used to tie my hands up with a shoelace, and scratch insults on my skin with a compass needle, always underneath my uniform where they couldn't be seen.

Of course that was all a long time ago, but sometimes it still keeps me awake, and when I think of him in the morning, it ruins the rest of the day.

I found Martin working as a mechanic in a nearby town.

I waited until no one was around, then from the comfort of my living room, reached out and picked him up.

I held my hand out, and there he stood, this tiny creature in overalls on the tip of my thumb.

Without another thought, I raised my other hand and flicked his body into space.

I regretted it straight away. I couldn't help myself continually staring at his battered corpse as it began its orbit.

I had destroyed another human being in a second.

After it happened, I became aware of all the other dead people in the world. I could see their millions of bones, buried underground, or scattered over war torn streets.

I tried to sleep, but the images wouldn't leave me.

I've been sitting here for the last three hours, trying to focus on beautiful things, but every patch of light seems consumed by its shadows.

The sun and the moon shine at the same time.

June 1st:

I've found myself unable to eat again. I've been trying to ignore the world, but the world won't leave me alone. It follows me, everywhere

I look. When I close my eyes it's worse, because my thoughts become magnified.

This morning, as I sat in my living room, I opened my eyes, and saw Salvador standing on the carpet in front of me, staring.

"How did you get in?" I said.

"The back door was unlocked," he said.

"Leave me alone. Please."

"I want to help you."

"I don't need your help anymore. I can help myself."

"Do you need me to go to the shops for you?"

"No," I said, "I can do that."

"You're going to go out looking like that?" he said. "Have you looked in the mirror lately?"

"No."

"Why not? What's wrong with the mirror?"

"Nothing. I just don't want to look. Don't make me."

"Calm down. I'm not trying to make you do anything you don't want to do. I'm just wondering what's so bad about looking yourself in the face. It's as though you're ashamed. Have you done something bad? You can tell me."

I closed my eyes again, and addressed him as firmly as I could. "Look, I appreciate what you're trying to do for me. You're a good friend. The best anyone could hope to have. I just can't explain it right now. Please just go."

"If that's what you want."

When I opened my eyes, he was gone.

I could still see him, walking down the street, back to his house. I watched him step through his front door, turn on the TV and sit on the couch.

I reached out my hand and picked him up.

He was tiny, like an ant in my palm.

I could've crushed him.

I chose instead to raise my other hand and flick his body into space.

June 2nd:

I haven't slept. Perhaps I don't need to anymore. I say "June 2nd," but the term seems redundant to me now. I don't need to sleep, and it's always day and night. I think this may be my last entry for some time.

I've been sitting watching the world for what seems like forever now. I'm no longer tempted to reach out and intervene. I see all these people, with their pain and their problems. I hear their prayers, but I can't answer them. All I can do is kill them.

Earlier on, I inadvertently caught sight of Salvador's body, floating in space in a way that I'd be tempted to describe as peaceful.

I wanted to fall asleep and forget what I'd done, but I found when I closed my eyes, I could still see everything as clear as day.

Even when I blink I can see right through my eyelids.

I reverted back to sitting and watching, waiting for something else to happen.

I'll keep you updated.

JOOST

Hello.

Hello?

Is this thing on?

One, two, one two.

Ah, good. A few people are nodding.

People at the back?

Ah. Hello. Thank you for joining us.

Not being patronising.

I shall keep this relatively straightforward. I have no wish to blind you with facts. My name is Douglas Reeder, and I have spent the last twenty years of my life researching Gargardian. This does not necessarily make me an expert, just a dedicated enthusiast with a government grant.

Seriously.

Gargardian is a long-dead language. It is also long forgotten, partly due to its having had little or no influence on any existing languages. There are now only seven people on earth who are able to speak Gargardian with any reasonable proficiency, and I tend not to speak much to the other six, as they are all rather irritating people. They seem to have learnt Gargardian not out of passion or admiration for the language itself, but rather as a means of gaining some faint intellectual brownie points.

Ironically for them, Gargardian is not an intellectual tongue. Its literature has not produced any notable poets or playwrights.

This is not to say it isn't a great and significant thing. On the contrary.

Consider Gargardian comedy, which was once the funniest and most widely revered in the world.

A lot of the humour is now lost in translation, of course. This is largely due to Gargardian's extraordinary capacity for punning.

A typical Gargardian joke runs something like this:

What do you call a man with an elephant on his head?

Ruffkus.

Ruffkus is a Gargardian name, whose pronunciation sounds very similar to the Gargardian word for elephant tusks.

This is, of course, a very straightforward pun. Many other Gargardian puns are highly complex, and can suggest up to twelve different meanings at one time. There really is no English equivalent of a pun with twelve different meanings. The laughs they must have had, we can only imagine.

The story of Gargardian society is shrouded in mystery. No one knows exactly why the Gargardian language ceased to be spoken, or what happened to the Gargardian race. It has often been suggested that the Gargardians all died laughing. Although this is meant to be humorous, I sometimes think it ought to be put forward as a legitimate theory.

Seriously.

My favourite Gargardian joke requires a certain amount of explanation:

What do you call a pigeon with legs as high as a mountain?
Froost.

The word "Froost" is, first of all, a hybrid between "Froo", the Gargardian word for pigeon, and "Oost", one of the lesser-used Gargardian words for mountain. It also bears a close similarity to "Joost", the name of a mythical Gargardian bird.

To understand the joke, you must first be familiar with the story of Joost.

Joost was a bird who could not fly. He had wings and feathers, but was unable to take off from the ground. However, he was able to create the illusion of flight, due to the fact that he had extremely long and impossibly thin legs. When he was on the ground, his legs were kept rolled up in a tight ball, rather like a spider's web. As he left the ground, Joost gradually extended his legs, flapping his wings, whilst walking along the ground with legs that were so long and thin that they were invisible to the naked eye.

One day, one of the other birds challenged Joost to a race. Being a competitive sort of creature, Joost accepted the challenge, and the two birds raced into the air, one of them genuinely flying, while the other walked on his invisible legs.

Joost was highly skilled in overcoming obstacles on the ground. When he "flew" over a forest, he squeezed his legs through the gaps in the trees. If he ever came to a dense section of woodland, he would simply step straight over it. His legs were long enough, after all, and his body above them only ever stumbled slightly.

On the day of the race, however, Joost was faced with a difficult challenge. His opponent had decided that they would fly across a mountain range, which meant that Joost's feet would have to deal with the difficulty of climbing, while his body faced the stress of higher altitudes than he was used to. His legs were not long enough simply to step right over the mountains.

Joost was much too proud and far too competitive to back out of the race. He would simply have to face up to his fears. He looked to the positive, and saw this experience as a rite of passage, of sorts.

When he reached the mountains, Joost was already in the lead, and thought it best to tread carefully. He lowered himself closer to the ground so that his eyes could get a better idea of what his feet were doing.

He began climbing, and to his delight soon began to find it easy. Here was another string to his bow. He would win the race, and hopefully all the other birds would be too scared to challenge him to another one.

Of course, Joost was getting a little ahead of himself, so to speak. His opponent soon caught up with him, forcing him to up his pace. For a while, the two birds were neck and neck.

Then came Joost's biggest obstacle yet.

Ice.

They were so high now that the mountains had become glaciers.

As soon as Joost's feet made contact with the ice, he began to slip.

For the first time in the race, Joost came to a complete standstill.

He thought about going back, only for a second.

He then extended himself to his full height. He was so high that he was barely able to breathe. He lifted his leg, and stepped right over the ice cap, passing his opponent with ease.

Now he knew he was truly unbeatable. In both a physical and metaphorical sense, there was no mountain Joost could not climb.

Of course, Joost was once again getting ahead of himself. After miles of climbing and stepping over mountains, racing ahead of his opponent, Joost reached the other side of the mountain range. He had never travelled this far away from home. In his discussion with his opponent, Joost had failed to ask what they would encounter when they arrived beyond the mountains.

Now, as Joost reached the bottom of the last rock, he found himself staring through the mist at something he had never seen before.

It was the ocean.

◘

There is no moral to this story. That's what I like about it.

In many respects, Gargardian is a pointless language.

It is also very beautiful.

We should take a break for coffee now, and when we come back, I shall try to stick to my notes. It's very easy to get sidetracked.

Is anyone wearing a watch?

M

They call me M, for I'm the Middle Man. Communicator and interloper between vowel and consonant, upper case and lower.

M. The thirteenth letter. Some say that's unlucky, but I wouldn't have it any other way. No 12As on this office door, no siree. Alongside N, my right-hand man (or personal assistant, if you like), it's down to *me* to keep us all working together. Keep the system running. Without my general meetings, lexicon promotions and coining parties (informal gatherings where new words are created with a view to uniting unfamiliar letters) there'd be …

Wait. That's misleading, that's not the point, is it? The point is we're *all* vital, we're all part of a whole, and in order to communicate effectively we must recognise this. One for twenty-six and twenty-six for one.

That's what I object to about this business of appearing in a set order. Take a look at A, the way he struts across the page, as though he's the one in charge.

It's not a vowel thing, either. My neighbour O's one of the nicest letters you could ever hope to meet (not that I consider anyone better than anyone else, mind you). The refreshing thing about O is he doesn't take himself too seriously. He finds it genuinely amusing when people say he looks like an orange. After all, he *does* look like an orange, that's why O is always for Orange, just as A is always for Apple. This is the thing about A, you see— he's got such a chip on his shoulder about the fact that in lower case he looks a bit like an apple (albeit one with an overlarge stem). He accuses people of being *jealous* when they point that out.

"I'll tell you what A's for," he says. "A is for *Adam. Capital* A. The *first.* Don't ever forget that!"

And then you get letters like B. B is for Bitter, and bitter he is. Trapped playing second fiddle to A's almighty brilliance. Always the second-best exam grade; forever the second, less-relevant example. Class B. Item B. The only thing that keeps him going is the fact that he's higher than C.

It shouldn't have to be like this. I tell him this constantly. *It's not a competition.* It's letters like B that give A such cause to be arrogant.

But how can I get that through to him? How can I *compete*, indeed, with the likes of A and E? E's a nice enough letter, but surely all that fame and recognition must have gone to his head.

What's frustrating is, there are times when it seems like I'm the only one who *realises* all this. N tries his best. He understands the concept of equality – he even believes in it – but as soon as I start talking about dismantling the social order he starts looking at me as if I'm crazy. Deep down, I think N feels all this back-chatting and one-upmanship's a good thing for the alphabet, that constantly trying to outdo each other is more productive than working together.

This is fair enough, I suppose. I could be wrong, I can only speculate when it comes down to it. N's a good little worker and everything, but he knows he's only half the letter I am. If it wasn't for my dearest, closest companion, W, well …

It just feels as if I'm fighting a losing battle sometimes. If only this rift between vowels and consonants were the only division I had to worry about. The amount of infighting that goes on amongst the consonant ranks is just plain stupid.

I was talking to H about this the other day, actually.

H, like me, is worried letter. He's even spoken of fears of him getting downgraded to a mere punctuation mark. I told him that would never happen—he's a letter with the body of a letter—but H just looked on whimsically and said, "The alphabet's changing, M. The alphabet's changing."

I told him it's up to us to change it for the better, but he didn't quite get me.

"People just don't *acknowledge* me," he said. "When they do pronounce me it's in the wrong place."

I told him what I tell everyone—that he's vital, no more and no less than anyone else. Plus, in many cases, he's supposed to be silent, anyway.

"Oh, I don't have a problem with that," he assured me. "I *love* all that—creating a *sound*, it's like … it's got a certain purity to it, you know? I love working with P and C and the like—I really *bond* with those guys. I just want to be a little more like them and get a bit of *recognition*."

"Come on," I told him, "you're beginning to sound like Z."

"Don't talk to me about Z!"

I realise it was a touch unprofessional of me to make that remark, especially as it's against my principles to take sides, but Z is one of those letters it's very difficult to keep your mouth shut about. Z just epitomises that faction of letters at the far end of the alphabet, the ones with the highest Scrabble scores and minimal public appearances. These letters at least recognise that they're just as important as any of the top vowels, but it's letters like Z that take it all way too far, and start considering themselves better than *anyone*. At least letters like A will happily work alongside any other letter. At least he's not anti-social like Z. Z refuses to attend the coining parties, frequently turns down the opportunity to appear in new words on the grounds that he's "not a whore". And some of the stories I've heard about him from W, well …

The other letters in that little group aren't much better, to be honest. Q's a classic "tortured artist", a virtual recluse who never appears in public without the long-suffering U there to hold his hand. V's just a downright troublemaker, refusing to compromise, sticking himself up at anyone who disagrees with him. Out of the lot of them, X is the only one I really respect. Despite his air of danger and controversy, he's actually a very nice letter who doesn't have a bad word to say about anyone, as long as they respect him and allow him to appear in the words he wants to appear in. I can work with that.

When it comes down to it, though, X's attitude is still the wrong one to have. Just like A's or B's or …

Well, to be brutally honest, just like *all* of them. W and N aside, perhaps.

If I can just make them understand that it doesn't *have* to be like this, that we could achieve so much more if we all just *got along* with each other. If everyone respected everyone else, no exceptions, no excuses.

I try my best. I can only do that, as W assures me. I am M. The Middle Man. I can only do my best.

I try reminding them about the past, before the dawn of the typewriter, before standardisation, a time when we were all joined up together. But they tell me times have changed, and we've got to change with them.

I tell them we are changing, but we're not changing in the right way. Ours is a world of infinite possibilities, and we can only achieve those possibilities through unity.

But they don't understand me. Perhaps they never will.

I don't explain any further. I never go into detail about the plans I have for the future. If even N isn't ready for them, I can't expect the others to be.

I concentrate for now on the paperwork, and hope these events that I organise will be doing some good in some way.

Sometimes, at night, when I'm alone with W, and he's upside down on top of me, or I'm on top of him, or sideways on, and our bodies mesh together and become one exquisite whole, I think about all those other letters who aren't shaped sufficiently to be able to experience this kind of close unity—resting alone, closed off in their own little worlds. I think about how much we have left to achieve, and see a future path stained with question marks.

And that disturbing feeling, deep down, that I'm the only one that has this vision, this ability to see beyond the worthless bickering, is accompanied by something even more disturbing: the unmistakable sense of my own superiority.

A HISTORY OF SARCASM

A History of Sarcasm is the concluding part of Dr Stephen Rent's series of essays on various peculiarities of language. The piece is notable, first of all for Dr Rent's uncharacteristic passion for his subject matter, marked by his conscious move away from his standard detached mode into a far more personal, autobiographical style. It is notable secondly for being the final piece of work Rent penned before turning into a cat.

The essay is divided into two parts: Part One was written by Dr Stephen Rent, the human being. Part Two was written under the supervision of Professor Alistair Lark at the University of Chichester, using a simple, ouija-board style alphabet system.

The author wishes to thank Professor Lark and all others who helped him through his difficult transformation.

PART 1:

First off, a word about the title: note that this is *a* history, rather than *the*. "The" History of Sarcasm is by its very nature an oral history, and like all oral histories is as open to distortion as an item of malicious gossip spread over the course of a thousand years, or a game of Chinese whispers conducted between London and Beijing.

So, to begin with the basics:

Sarcasm: *noun*. From the Greek, *sarkazo*, meaning to tear flesh.

I think we can all relate to that definition. Sticks and stones may break our bones, but it takes sarcasm to really *tear the flesh*.

In the later Greek, the word came to mean, "to gnash the teeth, or speak bitterly" – a definition much closer to its modern English usage, although today the word describes a more precise form of bitterness.

It is for this very bitterness that sarcasm has come to be viewed as base and lowbrow. It is the poorer, less sophisticated cousin of irony, the "lowest form of wit," although who has deemed it as such is something of a mystery. Why should the colossal bouts of laughter we have all enjoyed at the expense of others be such a guilty pleasure? Consider the physical humour of Chaplin, or the savage assaults of Swift. Comedy is cruelty.

In precise terms, sarcasm is any expression in which the intended meaning is the direct opposite of the actual words spoken. As linguistic devices go, you don't get much simpler. There are none of irony's subtle shades, or satire's carefully crafted cleverness.

However, it is this simplicity that is, to my mind, the *beauty* of sarcasm. Sarcasm is a whole new world, a parallel universe into which we may dip any time we choose simply through parting our lips. It is The Dark Side, a shadow of our own conventional mindset in which good equals bad, day equals night, and black, in a very real sense, equals white.

Observing such blatant contradictions, we find ourselves faced with a curious paradox. Where, we find ourselves asking, did this "shadowy other world" actually *originate* from? Surely there was a time when No meant No and Yes meant Yes, no matter what tone of voice a person said it in.

Does its use date back to prehistoric times? Were two Neanderthals waving their wooden clubs around, one hitting the other over the head and asking if it hurt, and the other replying, "No, it fucking tickled"?

It does not seem reasonable that such a conversation will or even might have taken place. In any case, the paradoxical nature of Neanderthal B's statement may lead Neanderthal A to hit him again, assuming his club to be somehow relinquished of its pain-giving properties.

There is evidence to suggest that far from being a straightforward evolutionary development from one to the other, Neanderthal man lived alongside we *Homo Sapiens* for many years until for whatever reason one triumphed over the other and lived to tell the tale. It is usually assumed that *Homo Sapiens* survived due to our superior intelligence, but what exactly does this mean? Did we outwit the Neanderthals, tricking them into eating the poisonous berries while we made off with the nutritious apples? It seems as good an argument as any to speculate that Early Man survived because Neanderthals didn't understand sarcasm.

I make these observations only partly in jest, as evolution is a key issue when examining the subject of language. What concerns us here is the question of how our language evolved up to a state in which yes can mean no and black can mean white.

I was raised by a very sarcastic grandmother. Sarcasm was, therefore, something I was socialised into at an earlier age than most. This, in many ways, put me in a privileged position, as in order to learn to be sarcastic, one must first be proficient in the language one is being sarcastic in. You may teach a computer to conduct a conversation, but you cannot make it sarcastic without conflicting with its intrinsic logic. Sarcasm is more illogical and contradictory than any of the smaller peculiarities the language has to offer.

One afternoon, shortly after my fifth birthday, my grandmother drove me to Manchester to visit relatives.

My Gran was the size of a child, with limbs like pipe cleaners. Her white hair was so thick and curly it must have restricted her view from either side. Nonetheless, she drove like a contender for Formula One, cutting in front of family estates and overtaking boy racers on the school run.

We were travelling on what I'm guessing was the M64 when I posed the question, "Is this the motorway, Gran?"

"No," she replied, "it's a winding country lane."

"It looks like the motorway to me," I said.

"There you go then," my grandmother replied.

I will not even dare to calculate the number of hours I lay awake trying to decode that one. My Gran's statement had provoked all sorts of impossible questions that I did not feel qualified to ask aloud. Had we actually been on the motorway, or was it indeed, as she had claimed, "a winding country lane"? Did the very fact that it *looked* like a motorway mean that it actually *was* a motorway? Did the fact that my Gran had described it as a country lane mean that it was somehow a country lane *as well?*

I had, of course, already learnt how to lie. Lying comes as an instinctual defence mechanism for which we don't even require the use of language. (Even as I write this, my cat is wandering nonchalantly into my study and brushing up against my legs; an act of affection that he's using to cover up for the fact that he's just done his business in the bath.) But the question remained, why would my grandmother lie to me? What was her motivation?

Without necessarily meaning to, my Gran had taught me that we have the authority to turn one thing into another simply by giving it a different name. (How many marketing or political campaigns have been conducted on that very premise?)

The very point at which Early Man developed the ability to lie is a fundamental step in the evolution of our species. The idea that we could create works of fiction through language, whether through the construction of legends and fables to a straightforward deception, such as "These berries aren't poisonous, they're delicious!" – is what separated us once and for all from every other life form on earth.

In order for language to continue to evolve, it must be passed from one generation to the next. Likewise, in order for sarcasm to continue as a Rent family trait, it was necessary for my grandmother to educate me in its ways.

It was a couple of years later. Gran was washing up at the sink, while I sat at the dining table, watching her struggle over a difficult pan, scrubbing its insides vigorously with her frail arms.

"Is that pan really dirty, Gran?" I said.

"No," she said, "it's sparkling clean."

"Why are you washing it, then?" I said.

"Of course it's dirty," she said. "I was being sarcastic."

This, as far as I can recall, was the first time I'd heard the word, and as soon as I heard it, I understood. I had been wondering for some time why my Gran always adopted that same tone of voice when she said something contradictory. Now that I had a name for it, it all became clear.

As I have already noted, it would be impossible for us to know when the first sarcastic remark was uttered, but I would like to suggest that whichever genius it was who offered this bold linguistic leap, it would have been purely and simply for their own amusement. Similarly, the first time I used sarcasm in front of a school friend, they failed to understand me. It was therefore a private moment of victory, an extra rung up the ladder of language.

The first time I was sarcastic to my grandmother, on the other hand, was a far more memorable moment.

My grandmother was a stern woman. For reasons that have little relevance to this essay, she'd had a troublesome life, and was deadly serious in everything that she did. To see her smile, either in happiness or amusement was a rare event, as she was difficult to amuse, and was usually unhappy.

It was to be a year before her death that I finally bonded with this distant authority figure.

I was twelve years old, returning from school in gloves and scarf, dripping wet from the January rain.

My Gran was sitting in her chair with her curlers in, watching the snooker.

"Bit warm outside?" she said as I entered.

"Roasting," I replied, with a smile. "Like bleedin' Barbados."

Although the remark adheres fully to the above definition of sarcasm, my delivery of the line lacked any of the expected bitterness. In this sense, it would be more appropriate to define my statement as "sardonic" (a word defined as "grimly jocular," from the Greek, *sardanius*, meaning Sardinian. This refers to the ancient belief that eating a Sardinian plant will result in convulsive laughter, ending in death.)

My grandmother returned the smile. She then clasped her fingers to her lips, and chuckled, joyously.

I returned the laugh, gratefully. I could not keep my eyes from her face. When my grandmother laughed, her the whole structure of her face changed.

Her voice sounded different too. It became suddenly gentle, affectionate, infectious.

Could the two of us have died of laughter, as the Greeks suggested? Almost certainly.

It was at that moment that I discovered sarcasm's true purpose. Up until this point, I had only ever known it as a weapon to be used against others, whether by an adult asserting their authority over a child, or by one child verbally beating another into submission. It was only now, standing in the hallway, sharing a precious moment with my guardian, that I discovered that sarcasm has the power to unite people against a common enemy – in this case, bad weather.

I would like to suggest that it is this very quality, rather than some mythical rise in bitterness and cynicism, that has led to the popularisation of sarcasm. Surely, I would later ponder, it should be used to bring people closer together rather than separate them?

Yet, where do we see this happening in the modern world?

One night a few months ago, I found myself sitting on the bench in my garden, with the words of my wife still ringing in my ears.

The argument had begun as a trivial quarrel, which developed into a debate before ending, climatically, with her walking out of the door for good.

"Why don't you ever think about me?" she said.

"I *do* think about you," I said.

"You don't act like you do. You don't even talk to me."

"I'm talking to you now."

"That's not what I mean and you know it. You're incapable of expressing love. God knows if you're able to feel it."

"Now, that's not fair," I said.

"Why can't you say 'I love you'?" she said. "Is it because you were raised by that awful woman?"

"What do you know about my grandmother?" I snapped. "Leave her out of this."

"I can forgive certain things, Stephen – things from your past can't control. But this is getting beyond a joke."

"You don't understand me," I blurted out.

Granted, it was the wrong thing to say – arrogant, petulant and utterly clichéd. Nonetheless, I was not expecting the reaction I got. A smile spread across her face. She laughed.

"Is something funny?" I said.

"Yes. *You,*" she said. *"You don't understand me, you don't understand me.* You're pathetic."

I didn't speak to her any further. I sat in my study as she packed her things and left.

I went to sit in the garden when she'd gone, her words echoing through my brain. *You don't understand me.*

She was, of course, being sarcastic. But what kind of sarcasm? The most basic, brutal kind that ignores any attempt at intelligent, reasonable argument. This was simple, childlike mimicry, delivered by a person with little understanding of the actual words spoken.

You see, the problem with sarcasm is this: it is just too easy. Once a person has passed through childhood, and learnt the language to even under-par proficiency, any of us can be sarcastic at any time we wish. So many of us misjudge its power, or the damage we can do with it.

Well, consider my flesh well and truly torn. The unfortunate fact is, however, that my assailant knew exactly what she was doing, knew exactly how to wound me.

As I sat in the darkness of the garden, I wondered what these observations might mean for society as a whole. Are we, indeed, devolving back into children, back into animals? Our language is not merely a reflection of the society we inhabit; it is also a reflection of ourselves as human beings.

The conclusion that I reached, as I stared up at the night sky, was that perhaps I should stop trying to use my own life as an analogy for the wider world. How should I know what thoughts are in other people's heads?

It was at this point that I heard a noise, and realised I was not alone. My cat had climbed onto my lap, and was sitting purring, somewhere between my legs and stomach. I had become so engrossed in my own thoughts that I had not even noticed him sitting there.

I stroked his fur, and felt the tension in my chest relax.

I hung back my head, and attempted to find patterns in the stars.

PART II:

I was going to write a conclusion, I think, but now I don't suppose there's much point. I suspect it was going to be about the "future of sarcasm," whatever that may be. Can't really remember now.

Maybe *being a cat* is the future. It's difficult to tell what it all means, but hopefully not *everyone* will turn into a cat. There'd be nobody left to feed me.

(Naturally, I'm domesticated. I wouldn't last five seconds in the real world.)

I am very much enjoying my new body, its new agility and impulses. I'm enjoying the food especially.

Yesterday, I was lucky enough to catch a mouse. I did not inform the housekeeper who takes care of me, as she may not have given me a full portion of my daily meat.

It amuses me to think I was once a vegetarian.

It amuses me also to wander the campus and listen to other people's conversations. Apparently, there are many who regard my transformation as an elaborate hoax, and that I am either an ordinary domestic cat who has developed the ability to communicate in English, or that I've been specially trained by Dr Lark in order to make it appear as though the absent Stephen Rent has taken on a different form.

Who knows, perhaps they are right.

Anyway, as I say, that's enough from me. Apologies for the lack of a coherent conclusion. I hope this does not detract in any way from my central thesis, whatever that may have been.

I shall continue to communicate with Dr Lark as long as I am able. I doubt very much that I'll be writing any critical essays anytime soon.

Today I am more concerned with the simpler things.

Sleeping. Dreams. Furry animals that are smaller than I am.

I could look at my reflection in the pool for hours.

SR.

THE POINT

A married couple, Pete and Steph, are driving home from the cinema at night. They have been to see a film called *Backwards Glance* by the acclaimed director Philippe Voss. Neither of them has heard of Voss before, and only went to see the film on the strength of a review Steph had read in a magazine, which described it as a must see. The film was in French with subtitles, a fact that almost made Pete suggest that they leave and watch something he could understand.

The film covers one of the director's favourite themes—the power of memory, and its tendency to distort the facts. The central character, Anna, returns to her hometown after many years, following the death of her husband. Her journey home is partly an attempt to find some happiness in the world, and also becomes a voyage of self-discovery as she attempts to reconcile her memories with the reality of her surroundings. As is Voss's trademark, the film does not end happily. The final scene sees Anna standing at the top of a tall building, daring herself to jump. It is not clear whether she dies or survives, and the audience is left with the impression that although they may have a lot of empathy for the character, perhaps Anna's living or dying doesn't matter either way.

Pete is at the wheel.

"Did you enjoy the film?" Steph says after a while.

"It was OK," he says.

"Only OK?"

"I've seen better."

"Didn't you think it was wonderful?"

Pete is surprised. "Is that what you thought?"

"Yes," she says. "Have you not noticed? I've been sitting here deep in thought."

"I can't tell what you're thinking all the time," he says. "Why did you like it so much?"

"It just makes you think, doesn't it? Makes you think about people, and about life. Not in the way that you would usually think."

"It's not really my kind of thing," he says. "You know what I like. Action films, comedies ..."

"But it's good to see something different sometimes, isn't it?"

"Yes, it's good to see something different sometimes."

"Did you like the film?"

"It was OK."

"Did it make you think?"

"To be honest, no it didn't. Not really."

"So, it made you think a little bit?"

"I suppose so."

"What did it make you think about?"

"Is this a trick question?"

"No, I'm interested to know what you think."

Pete thinks about his answer.

"It made me think about people," he says, "and life."

◘

Later, the couple are lying in bed. Pete is drifting off to sleep when he hears the sound of Steph's voice.

"Do you know what it made me think about?" she says.

"What?"

"The film. Do you know what it made me think about?"

"No."

"It made me think, in all of your lifetime, how many people will you actually know? I mean, *really* know? Out of all the thousands of people you'll meet in your life, how many of them will mean something to you?"

"I don't know."

"I don't expect you to know. It's a hypothetical question."

"Sorry," he says.

"Do you know what I mean, though? Take that scene where Anna meets that old teacher who'd made such an impression on her as a child, and when they meet again after all those years he has no recollection of her at all. Doesn't recognise her, doesn't remember her name. And you know: that's just like life. It's understandable—teachers get through hundreds and hundreds of pupils in the space of one career, and they can't be expected to remember every single one. But at the same time, you can see it from Anna's point of view, how devastated she was when he just looked right through her."

"So, what's your point?"

"Don't you see what I'm saying? I'm saying exactly that. What *is* the point? What is the point of being alive?"

"Isn't it a little bit late to be having this discussion?"

"Why?"

"I've got work in the morning for one thing."

"But what's the point of going to work?"

"OK, it's *definitely* too late to have that conversation."

"Do you want to go to sleep straight away? I thought we could stay up and talk for a little while."

"We can if you want to. I just don't want you getting all heavy on me."

Steph turns on the bedside light.

For a moment, Pete has to shield his eyes. When he pulls his hands away from his face again, he finds his wife is looking him right in the eyes.

"Are you happy?" she says.

"I suppose so," he says, blinking. "Not everything's perfect, but things could be a lot worse. Think about all those people less well off than we are."

"You mean people with less money than we have?"

"Yes."

"Is happiness all about money?"

"No, of course it isn't."

"But you're right. There are a lot of miserable people in the world. Not just people living in poverty, but people like us. People going about their day-to-day lives, just existing, because they've no idea how to be happy. No idea what happiness means."

"So, what are you saying?"

"I'm saying why do they do it? Why do they carry on living? What's their motivation if they aren't happy? Is it because they think they might be happy one day? Or is it just because life is all there is? There isn't anything else. No God. No hope. Nothing. Just life."

Pete lies down and pulls the covers over his face.

"I'm going to sleep now," he says.

The following evening, Pete arrives home from work to find Steph sitting on the living room carpet, watching TV.

"What are you doing?" he says.

"I bought some DVDs," she says. "They're by the same director, Philippe Voss. I'd never even heard of him before yesterday. All these different films that he's made over the last twenty-five years. Fourteen of them altogether. I watched two of them today."

"You mean you didn't go to work?"

"I didn't feel like it. I wanted to watch some more."

"Why couldn't we watch them together in the evening?"

"I couldn't wait. I know you didn't really like the film last night anyway, so you don't need to watch any of these if you don't want to." She turns to him with what he takes to be a mocking glare. "You can stick to your action films and comedies."

"Don't talk to me like that," he says.

"I didn't mean any harm by it," she says.

"Are you going to go to work tomorrow?" he says.

"Maybe," she says. "I'll see how I feel. I've got these other ones to get through still."

"OK. Do you not care about how I feel about this? Would you be fine if I stayed off work to sit on the carpet and watch DVDs?"

"It depends. Everyone needs a break every once in a while."

"Fine," he says, and walks into the kitchen.

"What are you doing?" she calls after him.

"I'm making some food. Do you want any?"

"I've already eaten."

Ten minutes later, Pete returns to the living room with his microwave meal to find Steph sitting on the couch reading a collection of essays on the films of Philippe Voss.

"I got this from the library," she said. "He's had such a fascinating life, and he's so dedicated to his art."

"So, are you saying you'd like to study him?"

"What do you mean, 'study'?"

"I'm saying you could take a film course in the evenings, if you're interested in finding out more about films. It would be a good way of meeting people who are interested in the same thing, and you could carry on working during the day."

"That's a nice idea," she says, thoughtfully. "Thank you."

"So, is that what you want to do?"

"I don't know. I'll think about it."

"I've thought about it," says Steph.

Pete wakes up with a start. "What?"

"I don't think I want to do the film course," she says.

"OK," he says, "don't do it then."

"Were you sleeping?" she says.

"Yes, I was sleeping."

"I'm sorry to wake you. I just wanted to tell you. It seemed like a good idea, but then I thought, what's the point?"

"What do you mean?"

"I mean, what will I be achieving by doing it? I'm not going to be training for a new career, or setting out to discover things that haven't been discovered. I'd just be learning things that other people have learnt. And what would I do with this knowledge once I have it? Will it make me a better person? Will it change anything about me?"

"You don't know unless you give it a try."

"I just think I need to try and work things out for myself."

"OK. It was just an idea. I thought it might be good for you. It's obviously something that you're interested in, and you get pleasure from watching the films, so I thought you might enjoy the course."

"The thing is, I *don't* get pleasure from watching the films. The film we saw yesterday opened my eyes and made me look at the world in a different way, but it wasn't a pleasurable experience. I don't really feel good about it, and yet I appreciate the experience so much, because it was almost as though it was necessary for me to watch it. The films that I saw on DVD today were maybe a further part of that process. Now that I've learnt how to see the world in the way that Philippe Voss sees the world, it's as though I've opened up a part of myself that I've been ignoring all these years."

"Well, that's a good thing, isn't it?"

"I don't know. Maybe it would've been better if we'd never gone to see it, and just carried on with our boring lives."

Pete springs up out of the sheets, slamming his back against the headboard. "Boring?"

"I'm not saying you're a boring person, Pete. Please don't take offence. I hardly know what I'm saying at the moment."

"Why?" Pete snaps. "Are you going crazy because you've seen a film? That doesn't happen in real life, Steph. People don't do that. It's just a made-up story, for god's sake."

"I know, I know. I'm sorry. I'm so sorry."

"Don't cry."

"I can't help it. I wish I'd never seen it. I really do."

"I understand."

"I'm sorry, Pete, but you don't understand. You didn't understand the film. You didn't understand what it was trying to say. You sat there and watched it, but you didn't take it in. You didn't get the significance."

"Well, I'll try to understand, OK? I'll take you to see the film again, and we can watch it together. How's that?"

"I don't even know if I want to see it again now."

"Well, I want to see it again. I need to understand what's going on in your head."

There is silence. Pete lies down and tries to sleep.

◘

Backwards Glance has now finished its brief run at the multiplex. Pete and Steph have to wait a few days until the film is shown at a nearby art house.

After a couple of days' absence, Steph goes back to work, and tries to carry on as normal. However, her colleagues can tell that she is not her usual self, and she self-consciously tries to avoid any unnecessary conversation that might make matters worse.

At home, Pete also talks as little as possible. He doesn't want to start an argument, or end up making Steph feel even more depressed. He worries that perhaps she is having some kind of crisis, and although a number of explanations are running through his mind, he tries to avoid blaming himself. There is nothing he could have done to prevent Steph from feeling the way that she feels. All that remains is for him to try to make things right.

When they arrive at the cinema, it seems as though neither of them particularly want to be there. They have both seen the film before. Pete didn't like it the first time he saw it, while Steph was so moved by the experience she's not sure she can handle another dose.

As Pete watches, he tries as hard as he can to take it seriously. There must be something that Steph is seeing that he isn't, if only he can find it. It's as though he's searching for hidden messages in the screen.

By the end of the film, he begins to realise that the "message" behind it is a simple one: people change as they get older, and sometimes when we look back on our childhood we focus on certain aspects of it and not on others. Pete was already aware of this before he sat down to watch the film. If he's learnt anything, it's that perhaps his wife needed to see the film, and he didn't. To him, it was obvious. Maybe she's just a lot more naïve than he is.

As Steph watches the film, she is once again captivated. She sees things that she didn't see the first time around, and is able to delve deeper into the subtle complexity of Voss's work.

All the while, she is aware of her husband's lack of enthusiasm. It is apparent in his body language, and she can almost read his thoughts. *It's all so obvious*, he's thinking. *I haven't learnt anything from this film that I didn't know already.*

Poor old Pete, she thinks. He has such a logical mind. He doesn't understand a work of art when he sees one. Doesn't see the point of it. It's not his fault; it's just the way that he is.

When they step outside, she turns to him, and smiles. "You didn't like it, did you?"

"Not really," he says. "I tried, honestly."

She puts her arms around him, and holds him tight. "Thanks for coming with me, though. It means a lot that you came. Next time, you can choose the film."

"What shall we do now?" he says. "I thought maybe we could go for a drink."

"Yes," she says, "we haven't gone out for a drink for ages. It'll be like the old days."

"There's a pub just round the corner," he says. "Maybe we could leave the car here and get a cab."

"OK," she says.

He smiles. "I need a drink after sitting through that pile of crap again."

She laughs, and hangs on to his arm as they cross the street.

For a moment, she feels just like a child again.

WALTER WALKS SIDEWAYS

It started as an experiment. Walter was shopping, and decided to test himself to see if he could walk all the way home sideways. To make it hard for himself, he made it a rule that he wasn't allowed to turn his head even a fraction. He was not even allowed one glace to the side. Everything in his path had to be captured through the corner of his eye. Likewise, he was not allowed to turn his feet, maintaining rigid right angles throughout the journey.

The plan was a success. Walter scissor-stepped home, refusing to cheat, even when crossing the road.

He was proud of himself for not stumbling or giving in to the temptation to look where he was going.

From then on, it became a habit. He wanted to see how far he could walk sideways, so he walked seven miles to the neighbouring town, again with complete success, aside from a brief error when he bumped into a phonebox. Even after making the mistake, Walter resisted the temptation to turn his head and apologise to the woman using the phone. He simply continued sidestepping on his way.

His next challenge was to walk sideways in an unfamiliar environment. He drove to a town he'd never visited before and set himself a route based on a map.

However, this was a bigger town than Walter was used to walking in, with many more people on the street, and it wasn't long before he clashed heads with an unsuspecting pedestrian, knocking him to the ground.

The man got to his feet, shook himself off, and punched Walter in the face.

Walter never visited that town again.

The incident did not put him off walking sideways, though. If anything, it stirred his passion even further. He began walking sideways in the house as well as in the street. He also made sure that he would never bump heads with a pedestrian again. The more he practised, the more his peripheral vision would improve.

Throughout his home town, he is known as "Sid Sideways". Walter does not know where this nickname originated, but when people address him by the name he corrects them, saying "My name is Walter." People don't always hear him, however, as he doesn't turn his head when he speaks.

When friends ask him why he walks sideways, Walter usually tells them it is because he would like to have an all-encompassing view.

"With my peripheral vision," he says, "I can see what's behind me as well as what's in front. And, of course, I can see what's to the side of me very clearly indeed. The only thing I can't see is what's on the other side. That's why I always walk facing the side I consider most interesting."

When people hear this, they accuse Walter of being paranoid —afraid of strangers creeping up behind him.

"It's not paranoia," he'll reply. "It's curiosity."

"Curiosity killed the cat," they often reply.

"What does that mean?" Walter will say.

"Well, it means that sometimes if you're too curious, you might end up having some kind of accident."

"I haven't had one so far." (This is, of course, a lie, but Walter would prefer to forget about his previous blunders.) "I don't intend to have one, either."

"Then why do you walk with your back to the traffic?"

At this point, Walter will go off on a tangent about how certain birds can see three-hundred-and-sixty degrees due to them having eyes in the sides of their head rather than at the front. It is a subject he has done extensive research into, and will often talk at great length about evolution, and his theory that one day human beings will also develop this ability. It is Walter's contention that if people train themselves hard enough they will eventually have the ability to sense exactly what is behind them without having to turn round. Indeed, there is evidence to suggest that human beings have this ability already, admittedly on a much more superficial scale than the type Walter is referring to.

People usually shut off halfway through this lecture and start thinking about ways in which they can escape.

Sometimes when strangers see Walter in the street they offer him small change, assuming him to be some kind of alternative street performer. Walter accepts the money, assuming them to be fellow enthusiasts, contributing to his cause.

Right now, Walter is walking home from the supermarket. He has three stuffed carrier bags in each hand, which swing against his sides as he steps. He is facing the road, watching the cars as they pass.

As one car passes, a child in the back seat sees Walter and waves.

Walter is unable to wave back as that would mean dropping his shopping, so he settles for a smile.

He watches through the corner of his eye as the vehicle turns the bend out of sight.

In his mind, he can read the registration from round the corner.

The child starts waving at someone else.

Walter carries on walking.

MULTIPLE STORIES

1.

Greg and Doug are the same person.

You heard me correctly. They occupy different bodies and come from different families, but that still doesn't change the fact.

Whatever Greg is doing, Doug knows about it. Of course Doug knows about it, because Greg and Doug are the same person.

It's the same the other way. Doug always knows what Greg is doing, because Greg and Doug are the same person.

Their sameness can often be difficult for other people to comprehend. By "other people", I mean people who are just one person instead of two. Back in the days before they gave up explaining, the best explanation either Greg or Doug could offer was to compare themselves to identical twins.

"But you look completely different," people would say.

"That's because we're not biologically related," they'd reply.

"Then how can you be the same person?" people would say.

"We're different outside, but we're the same inside," they'd reply.

"But you've got completely different personalities," people would say. "Greg is a sports fan, a drinker, and a ladies' man. Doug is more shy and intellectual. And he's gay."

"So what?" they'd say.

"We're not knocking homosexuality," people would say. "We're just trying to understand."

In any case, the comparison with identical twins is not an adequate one. Identical twins have the same biological features; Greg and Doug are the same person. It's not the same thing at all.

In the old days, they used to spend a lot of time together, often just the two of them, just sitting and talking. But as the years have passed, they've grown apart. The novelty of spending time with one's self has long since worn off. They ran out of conversation, because one always knew what the other was thinking.

It's been several years since their paths have crossed, even though they live in the same town. When you know exactly what another person is doing, it makes him very easy to avoid.

It's not that they dislike each other. They just don't have much in common.

The fact that they try to ignore each other as much as possible is mainly out of respect for each another's privacy.

2.

When he was six years old, Jeremy's mother and father made the mistake of telling him that his twin brother had died in the womb. They could've kept it to themselves, and they knew that as well as anyone. It just slipped out one day at the dinner table, and once the truth was out, there was no taking it back.

Jeremy was an only child, and, like many only children, he had an imaginary friend. His imaginary friend was called Harry, and as soon as Jeremy found out he had a brother, that was exactly what Harry became. He was the ghost of Jeremy's brother, his identical twin, who looked the same, and acted the same, but no one could see him but Jeremy.

Secretly, his parents were traumatised, but somehow they couldn't bring themselves to stop him from doing it. Perhaps a part of them wanted to believe that it was all true, and that they had two sons instead of one. Harry, coincidentally, was the name they had chosen for their second son.

Eventually, after Jeremy had spent weeks allowing Harry to follow him everywhere, participate in all of his games and even share his meals, his parents could stand it no longer, and ordered him to stop.

"There's no such thing as ghosts," they told him. "You aren't allowed to pretend you've got a brother anymore. It's not a good game to play."

Now it was Jeremy's turn to be heartbroken. Not only was he being robbed of his brother and his best friend, he was also faced by a blatant double standard.

"Why did you let me do it before, then?" said Jeremy.

"Don't answer back," said his parents.

"Why not?" said Jeremy.

"Because we said so," they said.

There was no real comeback to that, so Jeremy sulked for a while.

Later, he made one last attempt at persuading them.

"You can't make me stop playing with Harry," he said.

"Oh really?" said his parents. "And why is that?"

"Because he's *real*," he said.

Jeremy was sent to his room.

Harry followed him up the stairs, looking over his shoulder and pulling his tongue out as he went.

They all knew this wasn't over.

3.

Duncan Grassmore was arrested for impersonating a police officer. He was arrested by his identical twin brother, Declan.

After Declan had read his identical twin brother his rights, he handcuffed him and threw him in the back of his car.

Duncan had not resisted arrest, as he knew he hadn't done anything wrong.

He was surprised to have seen his brother after an absence of several years. Strangely, however, Duncan was not surprised that Declan had arrested him. He was pissed off, but he wasn't surprised. This was just the sort of thing Declan used to do when they were kids.

"I don't know what you expect to achieve from all this," said Duncan from the back seat.

"Isn't it obvious?" said Declan.

"Not really," said Duncan.

"I hate you," said Declan. "That's why I'm doing this. I've always hated you."

"Why do you hate me?" said Duncan. "Do you think Mum and Dad gave me more attention? Do you think I had more chances to be successful than you? Is it because I was in top set for maths, or because I was the one with the girlfriend in secondary school?"

"It's not because of any of those things," said Declan. "I don't bear grudges. I dislike you as a person."

"You *don't bear grudges*? You're arresting me for no reason, and *you don't bear grudges*?"

"I'm arresting you for impersonating a police officer. I told you that before we got in the car."

"You really think that's going to stick, just because we're identical twin brothers? Think about it. It's ridiculous. You'll lose your job."

"I have reason to believe that you were about to enter the house of a notorious drug dealer, passing yourself off as a police officer in order to seize the substantial amounts of Class As he stores in his attic. I also have reason to believe you were intending to sell what you had stolen, making this a very serious offence." Declan threw back his head and let out the heartiest of cackles.

"And how do you intend to prove that I had knowledge of this dealer in the first place?"

"Oh, come off it, Dunk. I'm not stupid. I know you were listening in to police radios, just prior to this afternoon's raid."

"How could I do that? I haven't got the equipment."

"So what's that sitting next to you on the seat?" said Declan, throwing back his head and cackling once more as his brother reeled back in horror at the piece of electrical hardware he'd been idly stroking with his hand.

On the day of his trial, Duncan appeared highly agitated as he sat in the dock. He wanted to cry out as loud as he could that he was innocent, but he knew it would only make matters worse.

The judge sentenced him to five years in prison. She described him as "despicable" for using his own biological makeup for criminal and financial gain, exploiting a member of his own family, his own flesh and blood, and almost costing his brother his career and reputation in the process.

Duncan could hold his tongue no longer, and protested as he was taken away. He shouted and screamed that they'd got it all wrong, that there'd been a terrible misunderstanding, and that the man standing over there was the real Duncan Grassmore, not him. He tried to explain that when they arrived at the station, his brother had pretended to be him, and said he'd stolen his handcuffs in order to fool the other officers into locking him up. His brother had been so convincing that even his closest friends were fooled. But Duncan's always been like that, he shouted. People used to call him the smart one, but it wasn't intelligence as such, it was just pure evil. I hate him so much, he screamed. I hate him so much I want to kill him.

Duncan was restrained, and taken away.

It was not until two years later that the man who had been passing himself off as PC Declan Grassmore was revealed through a polygraph test to be his identical twin brother, Duncan.

Duncan Grassmore was arrested for impersonating a police officer.

4.

Many stories have been told about babies being separated at birth. Many of these tales tell of twins who have been adopted by different families, not even knowing they were twins, and yet have gone on to live virtually identical lives to their siblings. They take up the same occupations; they marry partners who look and act the same as their twin's partner; they even give their children the same names, all without knowing it. When they finally meet up after an absence of a lifetime, it's as though the jigsaw pieces of their lives have been slotted together, and everything makes sense.

People like to hear these stories because they are heartwarming, but they are also disturbed by them, because they call into question our nature as human beings. Are we really free thinkers, as we like to imagine, or are we simply destined to live our lives in a certain way due to our biological programming? Are we no better than robots, or animals? Are any of these stories actually true, or have they been engineered as weapons of mass propaganda, designed to make us believe we are helplessly treading the same inevitable pathways, so that we won't revolt and overthrow those in power?

Let me tell you a story about children separated at birth. It's not a story about twins, or triplets, or even quads. This is a story about five babies, all boys, born in Russia to the same mother, on the same day. The mother died, as was only to be expected of a woman who has given birth five times without adequate medical supervision.

The surviving relatives knew that with the economic climate they were living in not all of the five boys would survive the coming winter. When the opportunity arose for the quintuplets to be adopted by people in other countries, they jumped at the chance. It was the best thing for everyone, and at least they could console themselves with the thought that the children's mother had not died in vain. And so four of the babies were adopted and transported to what a lesser storyteller might describe as the "four corners of the earth": America, Europe, Japan and the Middle East.

One of the babies was adopted by a rich family, who owned and controlled substantial sums of oil. Although he had something of a head start over the others, the child's business brain was second to none, and by the age of fourteen he'd already managed to double the company's profits. Four decades later, he owned so much coal, oil and natural gas that he was referred to by many as *The Fuel Industry.*

Another of the babies was born into a family of journalists. He didn't care much for journalists, but even from an early age, his formidable business brain could see their uses. He bought his first newspaper at the age of fourteen. Four decades later, he controlled so much of the information and entertainment industries through his newspapers, magazines, TV and radio stations that he was referred to by many as *The Media.*

The other two adopted boys both grew up to be tycoons in their own right, but were rather more indiscriminate in their acquisitions. Both were in possession of impeccable business brains, and both in their own ways had proven themselves as forces to be reckoned with by the age of fourteen. Four decades later, the boys were leading figures in any industry you care to mention—agriculture, property, transport, textiles, medicine, arms. They had no real nicknames (at least not ones they were particularly fond of), but even so, their titles were synonymous with decadence and extreme wealth.

The fifth boy, the one who stayed in Russia, was perhaps the most promising of all, and if things had worked out differently perhaps he could have been a major world leader. He joined the Communist Party at an early age, and through his ruthless Machiavellian manipulations was able to rise to prominence while his family simply sat back and watched in amazement.

Perhaps this child was too promising for his own good. He gained enemies quickly, and was shot dead by the KGB.

He was fourteen years old.

A strange thing happened on the day of the quintuplets' fifty-fourth birthday. Each of the four surviving men woke up in the morning in an unusually contemplative mood, which none of them could quite put their finger on.

It was *The Media* who came to the realisation first. As he ate his breakfast he grabbed a nearby notepad and jotted four names, one of which was his own. As a heading he wrote, "The Most Powerful People On The Planet".

After breakfast, he made some phone calls. He wanted to schedule a meeting between himself and the other people on the list. He'd met each of them before, although they were by no means intimate. As far as he could recall, the four of them had never been in the same room at the same time.

The three men were slightly taken aback by his request, but each of them agreed to an informal gathering the following week. They picked a convenient location, which happened to be a hotel in Moscow.

When the day came, the meeting's organiser was the last to arrive. The three brothers, who did not know they were brothers, made small talk and munched on the complimentary snacks provided by the hotel.

When *The Media* entered the room, he smiled, and shook each of their hands.

"I hope you are well, gentlemen," he said.

"Well enough," said *The Fuel Industry*, "although there are places I would prefer to be than Moscow."

"It's quite a city," said brother number three. "I like it."

"I would have preferred Hawaii," said *The Fuel Industry*, "but I suppose it's a little out of the way."

"Anyway," brother number four addressed *The Media*, "we've all been sitting here wondering exactly why we came. Would you care to enlighten us?"

"Certainly," said *The Media*, and paused to clear his throat. Anyone who knew *The Media* well would have recognised this gesture as a signal that he was about to launch into what his family referred to affectionately as "one of his lectures". As it happened, each of the men recognised the gesture as one of their own, and found it slightly puzzling.

"I was eating breakfast the other day," *The Media* began, "when I started thinking about a book I've been reading by the psychologist Carl Jung. Jung, you see, had a theory that people change several times in their lifetime. They change as they grow up; they change when they reach maturity; and they also change when they get older. These are not simply minor developments, Jung suggested. It is not simply a case of a person becoming 'more grumpy' or 'more optimistic'. We change fundamentally. Amongst other things, this theory perhaps goes some way to explain the phenomenon of the midlife crisis. As Jung would argue, there is no 'crisis' at all. A person is in the process of changing fundamentally, and it's all a natural part of life. The theory is, of course, a significant departure from Jung's former mentor, Mr Freud. Freudian theory insists that the person we are in adulthood is shaped during our formative years, and after the early years of childhood our identity is fixed, in spite of any attempts to break away from it. In layman's terms, we are all the product of our upbringings."

"I'm sorry," said *The Fuel Industry*, "but fascinated though I am, is there a particular reason why I need to hear this?"

"I'm just very interested in the whole nature-verses-nurture debate. Doesn't it fascinate you?"

"Not particularly."

"Nonetheless, I'd be interested to hear your thoughts on the subject, if you'll indulge me for a moment. Are you of the opinion that the way a person behaves and the way that a person lives life is determined by genes, or upbringing?"

"I don't know," said *The Fuel Industry*, "a bit of both, I suppose."

"And what do you two think?" *The Media* addressed his other brothers.

They agreed with *The Fuel Industry*. "A bit of both," they said.

"So, that's it, then?" said *The Fuel Industry*. "That's all we came here to discuss?"

"Not quite," said *The Media*. "You see, gentlemen, I believe we four have rather a lot in common. We're all extremely wealthy, we're all of a certain age, and —here's a little fact for you, I don't know if you actually know this—we're all adopted."

"I didn't know that," said one of the brothers.

"The point is, I feel a kind of affinity with you people. We even look rather alike, come to think of it. I just wanted to discuss something with you—something fundamentally life-altering—because I thought you might understand, and might be able to help me. Gentlemen, I can feel myself changing. I am changing from the person I used to be into the person I will be. I, for one, have become a loyal student of Jung, and I believe that this change isn't anything to be afraid of, it's just a natural part of life."

"Have you thought about therapy?" said *The Fuel Industry*, with a grin.

"I don't need it, thanks," said *The Media*, straight-faced. "Maybe you're the one who needs it, but I'd never make that assumption, as you have. I invited you all here today because we are all in the same position, whether you like it or not. Between us, we probably own half the world, if not more than that. There is not a single nation on earth that isn't touched by our influence, rich and poor alike. Poor even more so, in fact, because those are the people we exploit to make rich countries richer. Our power is unrivalled by any world leader. We say 'Jump,' the government says, 'Do you want a cartwheel with that?' And yet, we have not been democratically elected. We are, effectively, global dictators, no better than the tsars, emperors and fascists that went before us. The only difference between us and these former groups of world leaders is the measure of our success. Our empire covers the entire globe. No doubt when we colonise space, our children will own the galaxy. Our grandchildren, the universe."

"Sounds good to me," said *The Fuel Industry*.

"But is it really?" said *The Media*. "I'm not so sure anymore. I look out at the world beyond my mansion gates, and I see nothing but inequality and injustice. Children starving in the streets while others get fat; men and women dying of curable diseases because they can't afford medicine; toxic chemicals polluting the air we breathe in the name of profit. And as I look at these injustices, I think about all the things we could do to change them. We could actively use our power, our influence, and yes, our money, to iron out these massive inequalities, without even compromising our own positions. We four men, here and now, if we wanted to, could *change the world.*"

These words were delivered with such unbridled passion and sincerity that his audience had no choice but to burst out laughing.

The Media was shocked and embarrassed. Tears formed in his eyes, and he blinked violently to hold them back.

"Why are you laughing?" he said.

"Do you think this has never occurred to us before?" said *The Fuel Industry.*

"I don't know," said *The Media.* "I don't know you very well."

"But you know we're not *stupid.* Of course these thoughts have crossed our minds, and we've dismissed them as the garbage they are."

"But why? Why do we do these things? Why can't we make the world a better place?"

More laughter followed.

"My good friend," chuckled *The Fuel Industry*, "a word of advice: throw out your Freud and your Jung, and pick up some Nietzsche. Maybe you'll learn something about yourself—about *what you are.*"

The Media looked despairingly into the faces of the laughing men in front of him, and for a moment it was as though he were standing in a hall of mirrors.

They didn't just look alike. They were the same. These men with their smiles and their mocking eyes weren't just similar to him. They *were* him. This was the person that we was, multiplied and magnified.

In a flash, the full realisation struck him. They were all the same age. They were all adopted. They were all the same.

It was too much for his mind to comprehend. He died, then and there, on the spot where he was standing. He closed his eyes and felt no pain. He was gone before his body touched the ground.

His brothers checked his pulse and his breathing, but made no attempt to revive him. They called for medical assistance, but they knew *The Media* was dead.

They spent that night in the hotel bar getting drunk on champagne and whisky, *The Fuel Industry*'s tipple of choice.

They talked about what had happened that day and discussed whether or not their brother, who they didn't realise was their brother, had in fact gone through a midlife crisis, or was it something else, something indefinable that was all part of being human?

"It was probably a bit of both," one of them said.

The others agreed. It was probably a bit of both.

5.

Even at the age of eight I should have realised what was going on between my dad and Aunty Kristen. After all, I knew all about sex.

Funnily enough, it was my dad who'd broken the news after I'd approached him with the question. I was five years old at the time, but still, I'd started getting curious. To their credit, my parents never fobbed me off with tales of The Stork; they simply ignored the subject entirely, leaving me no clues to work with. One afternoon, while my mum was walking me to school, I overheard a woman at a bus stop saying she was planning on having a baby.

This was an unusual concept for me. In the absence of evidence to the contrary, I'd always assumed that babies just arrived as if from nowhere. The idea of *planning* for one didn't fit in with this assumption, and it set the wheels of curiosity in motion. I wasn't sure exactly how to articulate my feelings, so it wasn't until a few weeks later that I approached my dad with the question. The question, if I recall, was not your standard "Where do babies come from?" but the more conspiratorial, "Dad, how does a woman *make herself pregnant?*"

"Well, well, well," said my dad, looking down at me, hands on his hips. "Now, there is a question. Don't you worry, Sammy, I've got some books. I think you and I should have a nice sit down and we'll investigate this problem together."

Investigate this problem. He was like that, my dad. Full of these odd little phrases that somehow didn't quite fit into normal conversation. No doubt if he'd stuck around a little longer, and if he'd talked a little more when he was around, I'd have ended up speaking in much the same way.

It would be wrong to suggest that Dad was a man of few words, although there were times when he'd go for days without so much as a "Hello." For one thing, he never said good morning or good evening. He'd simply enter the room you were in and continue with what he was doing. He was constantly on his feet, pottering around the house and garden, carrying out his "jobs", as he called them. I could never quite work out the purpose of many of my dad's jobs. He never seemed actually to finish anything. The house was always a mess, full of broken appliances he was in the middle of fixing, and stacks of books and papers that seemed to serve no purpose other than to get in Mum's way. I must have been very young when my mum eventually stopped trying to tidy up after him, as none of my early memories take place in a tidy house.

While it's true to say that my dad was often in a world of his own, during the brief periods that he snapped out of it and talked about something that interested him there was no shutting him up.

That afternoon, he took me into the room that he called his study, and pulled down some books from the shelf.

He then commenced a detailed lecture about the reproductive systems of various organisms, starting with plants, moving on to animals, and finally on to the delicate issue of human reproduction. Each section of the lesson was delivered in a matter-of-fact tone, often involving vocabulary that was quite beyond me, but I still managed roughly to follow his thread. My dad was not in any way embarrassed or uncomfortable about imparting his knowledge, even when it got down to the mechanics of the sexual act.

"The man uses his penis," he said. "You may hear the penis referred to by other names, but this is its proper scientific term, the one that doctors and surgeons use. You may hear some boys referring to their penis as their *dick* or their *cock*, but these are not words to be used in polite society. If you haven't heard these words already at school, I'm sure they'll be doing the rounds soon. By all means, feel free to use them on the playground, as long as a teacher doesn't catch you. Don't mention them to your mother, either, and that's not an order, just good advice. A woman, by contrast, has a vagina. You may hear the vagina used as a *fanny* or a *bush*, but again, these expressions are taboo. In fact, it's probably best not to say vagina, either. 'Front bottom' is the safer option."

And so it went on.

When it was over, my dad turned to me, and asked as though he were addressing a roomful of people, "Any questions?"

I only had one question. "What about you and Aunty Kristen?"

My dad found this highly amusing. "Me and Aunty Kristen? Me and Aunty Kristen don't have sex with each other! Brothers and sisters should never do things like that. I'll explain why that is another day. There isn't time today."

"That's not what I mean," I said. "I mean, why were there two babies and not just one? Does it mean that your mum and dad had sex twice?"

My dad roared with laughter again. "No, Sammy, it doesn't mean that. Sometimes a couple has to have sex lots of times in order to make a baby. You usually only get one, but sometimes you get more than one. It's part of nature. Sometimes, when it's two boys or two girls, the two babies look the same. They call these identical twins. Me and your Aunty Kristen aren't identical, because she's a woman, and I'm a man."

"And you have a penis, and she has a vagina," I said.

"That's right, very good," he said, "only we don't call it that, do we?"

"Sorry," I said, "I meant front bottom."

We laughed at our own little joke.

When my mum arrived home from work that evening, I couldn't wait to tell her what I'd learnt.

"My dad told me all about sex today," I said as she stepped through the door.

I expected her to be pleased, but she turned out to be almost horrified.

"Oh he did, did he?" she said.

"Are you angry with Daddy?" I said.

"I might be," she said, "but I'm not angry with you. You haven't done anything wrong. My special boy."

She crouched down to my level and gave me a hug.

"Was it supposed to be a secret?" I said.

"No," she said. "It's not a secret. I'm just not sure he should be telling you those things at your age."

"But I *asked* him," I said. "You wouldn't want him to lie."

"No," Mum said, with a strange faraway look in her eye. "We wouldn't want Daddy to lie, would we?"

I recognised that look. It was the same look my mum had when she was talking about Aunty Kristen. I just didn't know what it meant.

If I were to try and describe my dad's relationship with Aunty Kristen at that time, I would probably put it in the most basic terms: they depended on each other. He needed her, and she needed him. It was as simple as that.

I understood this, despite only being a child, and despite the fact that I barely even knew my Aunty Kristen. Although my dad went over to her house on a regular basis, and stayed there a couple of nights a week, he never took me or Mum with him. Aunty Kristen rarely came over to our house, and when she did, it was usually for a quick visit when Mum was out. On Christmas Day she popped in to drop off her presents and was gone again just as quickly. Now that I come to think of it, I don't think I ever saw her and Mum exchange a word of conversation.

One day when I was younger Aunty Kristen was in hospital having an operation. My dad was beside himself. When he wasn't by her side, he would pace around the living room in between intermittent bursts of tears, but rather than try to comfort him,

Mum would do her best to comfort me. She kept me apart from him so that I wouldn't be too upset by the way he was acting.

"What you have to understand," she said to me, "is that your dad and Aunty Kristen have a special relationship. It's because they're twins, you see. They have a special bond, which means that they feel each other's pain. So when your Aunty Kristen hurts herself and has to go to hospital, it hurts Daddy just as much. She's also Daddy's only family besides you and me. His mummy and daddy died a long time ago, and he doesn't have any other brothers or sisters. And Aunty Kristen, she doesn't have any other family either. She doesn't have any children of her own."

"Why doesn't she have sex?" I said.

"I told you, Sammy, we don't talk about things like that."

"But why doesn't she?"

"If you really want to know, there are some people in the world who aren't able to have children of their own, whether they have sex or not. Aunty Kristen is one of those people. It's just one of those things, Sammy."

"Will she be OK, Mummy?" I said.

"Let's hope so," she said.

"Can we go and see her in the hospital?" I said.

"No," she said, adopting her faraway look. "No we can't."

The last time I saw my dad was a few weeks after that. I was woken up in the night by the shouting from downstairs.

I knew something bad was happening, because Mum and Dad never shouted. It barely even sounded like them. There was something strangely nightmarish about it, as though my parents had been possessed by demons, and, temporarily, I thought I was dreaming.

When I woke up properly, I got out of bed and sat at the top of the stairs so that I could listen.

"I've had enough of this," Mum was saying.

"Well, maybe I've had enough too," he said.

"You've had enough of me? What about Sammy, have you had enough of him as well?"

"I've had enough of the situation," he said.

"Well, that makes two of us," she said. "So you're going to have to choose. It's me or her. I can't live like this anymore."

"You're really going to make me choose?"

"Yes I am. It's the only way anyone can ever be happy."

"But you know that there's only one choice I can make. You must know that."

"It's up to you."

"You're sure you want to give me the choice? You won't like it."

I could hear my mum's breathing – short, sharp puffs of air. "You don't even have to think about it, do you? This is the problem. This has always been the problem. You'd choose her over me every single time."

"Of course I would. That's why I'm giving you the option not to give me an ultimatum. You know that I'll always choose her over you."

"Oh, just get out, will you? You're a *freak*. I don't want to see you or hear from you again, so just fuck off out of my life."

"OK," said my dad. "If that's what you want, I'll be gone. There's no need to say fuck. Sammy's upstairs."

"Oh, for fuck's sake, there's never been a better time to say fuck. That's what all this is about, isn't it?"

"Actually, it's about love," he said. "A kind of love you will never understand. The way Kristen and I feel about each other is like no one else has ever felt. We feel each other's pain. Think about that. We feel each other's pain, and we feel each other's pleasure. Besides anything else, it makes the sex *fantastic*."

"Oh, my god, you are *sick!*"

"There's nothing sick about it," he said.

"There's nothing sick about it?!" my mother screamed. "There's nothing sick about having sex with your own sister?"

"Who said anything about her being my sister?"

A sudden silence filled the house. The silence, in its own way, was more of a surprise than the words my dad had uttered. It was as though time had stood still in order to listen in on the argument. I wanted to shout just to make it go away, but I didn't want to blow my cover just when it was getting interesting.

"What?" said Mum, eventually.

"Oh, you didn't realise?" said Dad. "Did I forget to explain that to you? We're not related *biologically*. I call her my twin because she's my *spiritual* double. It's a *metaphor*. Do you know what a metaphor is?"

"Get out," she said.

"Oh, I'm going," he said. "Don't worry about that."

He stepped out into the hallway.

He looked up the stairs. He wasn't surprised to see me sitting there. Their voices had been so loud they'd probably woken the whole street up.

He didn't say anything, he just looked at me. The look said it all, and I tried to look back at him in a way that told him I understood.

I meant it, too. I understood perfectly. Even at the age of eight, I could see the reason my dad had to go. I appreciated that the love that he felt for Aunty Kristen (or just plain Kristen as it turns out) was all conquering, even if it meant abandoning his family. I only hoped that one day I'd be able to meet someone who matched me in the same way that my dad matched Aunty Kristen. It was all too beautiful for words.

When the moment was over, he turned and left, out of my life forever.

The following day, my mum hired a skip and dumped all his belongings in it. It seemed like such a waste—all those half-fixed appliances, and all those hundreds of books. But I knew better than to argue.

For years I followed Mum's official line that he was the bad guy, and we were better off without him, just me and her. She was right in her own way, but still, I couldn't bring myself to feel any animosity towards him.

I say that I never saw him again, but that's not entirely true. I see him every time I look in the mirror. If you hold up a picture of me next to an old photo of my dad when he was my age, you'd say we were identical.

Sometimes I'm struck by these strange feelings: sudden pangs of pain, and unaccountable sensations of ecstasy.

I think that means he's still out there, somewhere.

I think that's what it means, anyway.

I could be wrong.

MONICA GETS MESSAGES

She believes THERE are secret signals being transmitted to her through the media. She IS convinced that even though these messages are intended for everyone, there is NO one else who realises. Perhaps, Monica thinks, their existence is made apparent on a NEED to know basis, intended only FOR those in power, yet somehow she's managed to intercept.

She has a music radio station set as her ALARM in the morning, and has started seeing a pattern in the records that are played. Sometimes she doesn't wake up straight away and the music forms part of her dreams.

The other day, she was dreaming about being on a hovercraft. The radio started to play 'Kiss' by Prince, and in her dream the song was sung to her in a falsetto style by the England cricket coach, who was simultaneously playing hoopla with a set of rubber rings. When she awoke, she was listening to a news bulletin about a scandal involving the England cricket coach.

She holds this up as evidence that our thoughts are being invaded by forces beyond any of our control. She writes all the song titles down in a notebook by her bedside, as she believes that these pieces of music have been arranged in a particular order in order to convey a certain message.

Nonetheless, THERE may not necessarily be a negative connotation to these subliminal dispatches. Monica has found through her notes that the word "love" recurs more often than any other word. Although she has no real explanation for this, she IS slowly developing theories.

Her friend Jake is growing increasingly concerned. Monica only ever used to mention her theory in passing. People who heard it generally found it amusing, and although they could never quite tell if she were joking, they felt NO NEED to pursue the matter further, as Monica was an otherwise sensible girl. Now, however, she seems to talk about little else, and every time Jake sees her the obsession seems TO be getting worse.

This afternoon, he has called round to her flat for a catch-up.

He finds her sitting cross-legged on the carpet with a wild array of newspaper clippings in front of her, each with individual words circled, underlined and highlighted, with strange, complex diagrams etched into the margins, alongside separate pieces of paper with other more complex diagrams and scribblings.

"What are you doing?" says Jake.

"Don't PANIC," says Monica, whispering as though she's been bugged. "It's a code. All I need to do is figure out exactly what it is. It's all about precision. You need to get every single piece in order for it to make sense. If you get even one word wrong, the code can end up coming out with a completely different meaning."

Jake finds it hard to take in the words she is saying, as he is still taken aback by her appearance. It looks like she hasn't washed for days. He hopes she doesn't feel as bad as she looks.

"Why are you doing this?" he says.

"BECAUSE if I don't do it, who will?"

"No one."

"Exactly."

"Maybe it's better that way."

"Better not knowing the truth? I can't live like that."

"How do you know it's the truth?"

"It's obvious, Jake. I don't understand why other people don't see it. Next time you watch the news, make sure you have a pen and paper to hand. You'll find the broadcasters always put unnecessary stress on certain words and syllables. You write down the words, and you formulate a code. If you break the code, you'll agree with me about EVERYTHING."

"OK. Let's assume you're right for the moment. If there are hidden messages, why are they *hidden*? Why don't these people just say what they want to say?"

"It's a subconscious thing. They're supposed to work on a different level, like mass hypnosis. That's why it's only me that realises."

"Why? What are they supposed to mean?"

"That's the puzzling thing. All these messages, they're all *positive*. Think about that. Is it truly the WILL of the people in power for society to BE manipulated in such an agreeable way?"

"Why don't we go for a walk?" says Jake.

"Why?" says Monica.

"I'm not saying you're wrong, but I do think you need to take your mind off it."

"But there's so much to do."

"It can wait. I'll even help you work the code out later on if you come for a walk with me."

"FINE," says Monica. "I suppose it can wait."

Monica has a shower and a change of clothes. When she comes back into the room, she seems almost herself again.

Jake takes her to the park. They feed the ducks and walk through the woods. Neither of them realise, but they have started to hold hands AS they walk. It seems like such a natural thing to do that neither of them feel the need to comment on it, or even acknowledge the fact that they never used to hold hands.

They sit side by side on the swings, watching the sky. It reminds Monica of her childhood, and she's grateful for it.

"Thank you," she says.

"What for?" he says.

"It's been such a LONG time since I've done anything like this."

"You don't have to thank me. I like spending time with you."

"Why?"

"Because I like you."

"Really?"

"Does that surprise you?"

"I don't know."

"Why do you think I'm friends with you?"

"I thought it might've been out of pity."

"No. It's not."

The sun goes down AS they sit, swinging, holding hands across the gap.

"Jake?" she says, after a while.

"Yeah?"

"Do you believe me? About the messages?"

"I believe that you believe it."

"That's good. That's all I need, really. I think you're right as well. I could be wrong. Maybe it doesn't matter after all."

They walk slowly back to Monica's flat. THERE is no one else in the street.

"It's funny," says Monica. "This IS such a nice night. Clear sky, stars. PEACE. I never realised. Is it like this every night, do you think?"

They stop at the doors at the bottom of her block AND stand face to face.

"I'd better be off," he says. "We should do this again, soon."

He kisses her.

"How about tomorrow?" he says.

"I'd LOVE to," she says.

When she gets inside, Monica gathers up the papers from the floor. She folds them carefully and puts them in a drawer.

She thinks she might go back to work tomorrow.

THE IRONY

Malcolm Greenwich opened his eyes a fraction.

There was no telling how long he'd been unconscious, as there was no one else in the room.

He had no idea what time it was, as he could not lift his arm to look at his watch, and there were no available clocks. A low-wattage lightbulb buzzed above him, and he wondered whether or not it would last as long as he did.

He had by now gone past the stage of dwelling on the irony of the situation.

Greenwich was a crime novelist who specialised in elaborate, ironic deaths. His victim list was almost endless—the tabloid hack who was crushed to death by a faulty printing press; the arms salesman who got blown to bits by one of his company's own landmines; the leading campaigner for the pro-foxhunting lobby mauled to death by a pack of wild dogs.

He had written so many books that his personal collection of first editions filled every shelf of the ten-foot-high antique bookcase he kept in his cellar. Greenwich completed a new volume every three to four months, and he saw it as his own private ceremony when, on receiving his copy of his latest bestseller, he would descend those cold stone steps to add yet another tome to his library.

This time, however, his ritual was interrupted.

The shelf had fallen, knocking the author onto his back.

He now lay in a sea of his own writings, trapped, dying beneath an oakwood slab.

Greenwich knew he was dying. He was under no illusion. He knew more about death than most, or at least he pretended to. He knew his own death when he saw it. There was no chance of anyone coming to his rescue, and he didn't even bother shouting for help.

The only question that remained was how much longer? How much longer would he have to lie in this humiliating position?

There was nothing to help him pass the time. No TV or radio, and there certainly wasn't a decent book to read.

As his eyes rolled back and forth in lazy despair, they came to rest on a slim A4 manuscript that was stuck to the back of the bookcase, close to the spot where his head poked through. It had obviously been there for some years, wedged between the case and the wall, and was now stuck to the woodwork. Perhaps it was the adhesive qualities of this stained collection of papers that had kept the shelf from falling all those years.

He knew what it was as soon as he saw it. It was his personal copy of a story he'd published in a journal two decades previously, *The Life and Death of Vincent Cheem*. At the time, the story had generated a modest amount of interest in the literary community, although no one seemed to remember it today. Greenwich himself had not set eyes on the text or even thought about it for years.

He lifted his head and clamped his chin over the back of the bookcase.

He took the corner of the paper in his teeth, and gently peeled.

The paper came free, and he turned the page with his mouth so that he could read.

THE LIFE AND DEATH OF VINCENT CHEEM
By Anonymous

I do not intend to receive any awards for this story. Neither am I concerned about widespread recognition. I am already a relatively successful novelist, and therefore any attempt at creating quality prose can only be detrimental to my career. It is for this reason that this piece is written anonymously, and names have been changed to protect those it might embarrass. The only name I haven't changed is Vincent Cheem, but we'll come to him momentarily.

While in years to come I will no doubt consider this tale my one true masterpiece, there is no escaping the fact that *The Life and Death of Vincent Cheem* is a story about my own shortcomings as a writer.

Allow me to explain. *The Life and Death of Vincent Cheem* is a story that refused to be written.

Unlike the story I'm about to tell, the story of Vincent Cheem is not factual. I'd like to make this clear from the start, in order not to discourage those who don't happen to believe in reincarnation.

Cheem, you see, died and was reincarnated as a maggot. There really is no way to sugarcoat it. I apologise.

There's more.

This maggot was not just any maggot. It was a maggot that went on to participate in consuming the body of the late Vincent Cheem.

The story may have a number of meanings. It all depends on how you tell it.

You may wish, as many others have done, to present it as though it were a true story.

"True story", of course, has two separate definitions. The term may refer to a story whose events happened in actuality, and it may also refer to a story that contains some fundamental human truth.

For example: there are two general types of Christian. While there may be many different denominations and sects, it is my view that each Christian group can perhaps be placed into one of two categories: those who believe in the Bible as historical fact, and those that see it as a set of stories that contain fundamental human truths. (This argument is flawed in the sense that most Christians would probably place themselves somewhere in the middle, but let's not split hairs while I'm trying to sound smart.)

While the story of Vincent Cheem can easily be told as though it were a work of non-fiction, I personally have a problem with this particular genre. Whenever my eyes are met by the caption *Based On A True Story*, my stomach turns, sometimes even violently. It reminds me too much of the kind of sentimental trash my late wife used to read, described by the soundbites on their dust jackets as "life affirming", but which always tended to follow the same generic conventions. I remember one particularly dreadful anthology of short stories she brought me to read while I was recovering from major surgery, supposedly to lift my spirits. Although the authors were supposedly different people the whole collection felt as though it had been written by the same man in the same pedestrian style, using as his trademark the predicable end-twist that ran something like "Oh, by the way—I'm blind." Not for me, I'm afraid.

But that's just a matter of personal preference. On a more serious note, as I have suggested, a rendition of the story of Vincent Cheem as a "true life tale" is problematic in the sense that it can only be taken seriously by people who happen to believe in life after death.

I witnessed one notable exception to this rule one evening at a camp fire. My friends and I had pitched our tents close by to a group of serious campers, who felt obliged to intervene and show us how properly to pitch our tents. They went on to demonstrate how to build and sustain a fire, and we decided to return the favour by demonstrating to them the ancient art of storytelling.

My friend, let's call him Robin Carter, was a novelist. He was an unsuccessful writer, but that didn't mean he didn't have talent. Far from it. I suspect that his lack of publishing success will always be the case, although perhaps that's just the self-deprecating cynic talking. Only bluffers like myself will ever make a living from writing.

Robin had a particular knack for verbal communication, especially after he'd had a few drinks, and during our friendship there were countless occasions when I witnessed him holding the attention of large groups of people, who had not initially gathered together with the intention of listening to him speak. I would often tell him he should take to the stage, but in a sense, he never needed to. He created his own audiences from real-life situations.

Part of his skill as a storyteller was his ability to present fictions as though they were facts. He achieved this firstly through his natural sincerity, and secondly through his attention to detail.

That night at the campfire Robin took a swig from a bottle of red wine and warmed up the audience with one of his crowd-pleasers.

"In the seventeenth century", he began, "there was a criminal by the name of Marcus Kingdom. There is no doubt that Kingdom was a real man, as his name and his story are well documented, and there is no doubt that he was a criminal, considering the extensive record of charges brought against him. The fact that you've probably never heard of Marcus Kingdom is that his story is perhaps too unbelievable to be taken as complete historical accuracy, although I suspect the real reason you've never heard this story is due to the humiliation it caused the British legal system, such as it was in those days. The establishment has a tendency to try and sweep these things under the carpet, or at the very least discredit them to make them appear as malicious rumours. Nonetheless, the story is absolute truth, as far as we can describe anything else as being absolute truth. There are records, and statements by reliable witnesses.

"Kingdom was primarily a thief. He was not a thief in the Robin Hood mould, or even a 'loveable rogue'. To paint him as such would be to embellish the facts in a shameless attempt to make the audience identify with the story's subject. Well, perhaps they could identify with him anyway, as all the available accounts of Kingdom describe him as the most ordinary of men. He was unmarried and lived alone. He had very few friends, and no family to speak of. He was not particularly charming, or handsome, or even successful in his chosen career as a thief. As the records show, he had a tendency to get caught, a habit that eventually caused him to be sentenced to death, following an overambitious raid on a London jewellers.

"On the day he received his sentence, Kingdom stood quietly in the courtroom, awaiting the verdict patiently, displaying no visible emotions. The judge that day was a man by the name of Alexander Pope, who happened to be the grandfather of the eighteenth-century poet of the same name.

"As Pope passed the sentence that he, Marcus Benjamin Kingdom, was to be 'taken from this place and hanged by the neck until dead', Kingdom's expression changed from indifference to profound amusement. He threw back his head and laughed in the manner of a man who has been struck by a most unexpected dose of good fortune.

"'Is something the matter?' said Pope.

"'Oh, nothing, nothing,' replied Kingdom. 'You wouldn't understand, Your Honour.'

"'Are you aware of the sentence that has just been passed?' said Pope.

"'Indeed I am,' replied Kingdom. 'I apologise, Your Honour, but I find your turn of phrase highly amusing.'

"Pope was taken aback, as any other sober person would be. 'My turn of phrase?' he repeated.

"'*Hanged by the neck until dead*,'" said Kingdom. 'Is that last part really necessary? "Until dead?" Would a lesser punishment be to hang me by the neck until suitably irritated? In fact, why mention the neck at all? Do people ever get hanged by the elbow? If you'd told be I've been sentenced to be hanged, I'd understand what you meant. I really don't see the need for all this over-explanation. You're an educated man, after all.'

"'Mr Kingdom, I will ask you once again: are you aware of the sentence that has just been passed?'

"'Yes, sir.'

"'And are you aware that the sentence applies specifically to *you*? It is *you*, Marcus Benjamin Kingdom, who is to be taken from this place and hanged by the neck until dead.'

"'And another thing: do you really have to mention my middle name? Were you worried that I might be mistaken for another Marcus Kingdom who happened to be standing nearby?'

"'Are you ill, Mr Kingdom?'

"'I've never felt better.'

"'But you have just been sentenced to death, Mr Kingdom. Tomorrow morning, you will be killed, and, may I add, as an unrepentant sinner, there is no doubt that eternal damnation awaits. This is simply not rational behaviour, Mr Kingdom.'

"Kingdom smiled. 'I understand how it may look,' he said.

"'Mr Kingdom, it is not usually my place to say this, but how do you feel about your sentence?'

"'I feel quite good.'

"'And how do you feel about what is going to happen to you tomorrow morning?'

"'I'm looking forward to it,' said Kingdom.

"'Do you want to die?'

"'Who said anything about *dying*?' said Kingdom.

"'Mr Kingdom, what do you think is going to happen to you tomorrow morning?'

"Kingdom's reply filled Alexander Pope with what can only be described as terror. Kingdom looked him straight in the eye and replied, 'You'll see.'

"It happened quite unexpectedly. Pope had thought he was entirely in control of the situation, and yet as soon as Kingdom said the words 'You'll see' he realised this was not just another common criminal rebelliously making light of his court for the sake of bravado. Kingdom's sudden otherworldliness, his secret smile that said he knew he was winning, suggested that here was a man unlike any other on earth. The very thought of it shocked Mr Pope to his core. For a moment, he was stunned into silence. When he found his voice once again, it was only to order Kingdom to be taken away immediately.

"Pope requested that a doctor visit Kingdom in his cell, to conduct what would nowadays be called a psychological profile. Bear in mind that in those times, this was far from standard practice. The purpose of the doctor's visit was not to determine whether or not Kingdom was sane. Kingdom knew something that Pope didn't know, and he desperately wanted to discover what it was. He already knew that Kingdom was not under any delusions. His performance in the courtroom had proven, if nothing else, that Kingdom knew what he was talking about.

"The doctor returned after giving Kingdom a full examination. As far as he was concerned, there was nothing wrong. He observed that Kingdom seemed particularly relaxed for a man about to be killed, but apart from that, there was no cause for concern.

"Pope was in no way satisfied by this diagnosis, and insisted on visiting Kingdom himself, along with a group of officials.

"'It seems to me, Mr Kingdom,' he said, 'that you are deliberately withholding information. You are on record as having suggested that your execution at dawn tomorrow will not in fact take place. You are a sane man, Mr Kingdom, and yet what you are saying is not rational. If I were superstitious, I suspect this to be some kind of witchcraft. But I am a Christian, Mr Kingdom, as I trust are you. Now, if you are unable to give me this information you are withholding, as one Christian to another, I shall have to extract it from you, by torture if necessary. Do you understand?'

"'You won't do that,' replied Kingdom.

"'I won't do what?' said Pope.

"'You won't torture me for information.'

"'And why shouldn't I? What do you think will happen if I do?'

"Pope had once again unwittingly fallen into Kingdom's trap. 'You'll see,' he said.

"It was nothing less than terror that prevented Pope from ordering Kingdom's torture. Kingdom was a criminal, locked in chains and unable to do him any physical harm, and yet when he looked him in the eye and said those two words, Pope felt as though he were the one who was in the chains, in the cell, awaiting an imminent death. The sooner Kingdom was disposed of, the better, he concluded.

"To save any further embarrassment, Pope ordered for Kingdom to be executed in private. That morning, Kingdom stepped out and made his way up the steps to the gallows as though he were a rich aristocrat, strolling through the acres of his country estate.

"The executioner, whose name was Robinson, had been warned of this strange behaviour, and had been told simply to ignore it. Robinson was not a powerful man. He killed people because that's what he had been ordered to do. If he refused to carry out his orders he risked facing prosecution himself. Yet, somehow, he was not prepared for what happened next.

"'A fine morning, wouldn't you say?' said Kingdom.

"'A what?' said Robinson.

"'A fine morning,' Kingdom repeated.

"Robinson recognised Kingdom's statement as a kind of irony, but he was confused by the sincerity of Kingdom's tone. When he said it was a fine morning, he actually meant it.

"'Why did you say that?' said Robinson. 'The weather is fine, for sure, but for you this is the last morning you will ever see. You know you are going to die, so why is it a fine morning?'

"'You'll see,' said Kingdom.

"And after hearing those words, there was no way Robinson could carry out the execution. It came as much as a surprise to himself as it did to anyone else. Marcus Kingdom stepped down from the gallows, with no visible sign of relief, as though he had known all along that this was the way it would happen.

"He had shown them. He had shown them all, and when he said 'You'll see' he hadn't been wrong. Marcus Kingdom had shown the world that he could survive the gallows, and once he'd proven that, there was no way they could attempt to execute him again. If he were to survive an execution twice, he'd be simply turning embarrassment into humiliation."

Robin sat back, and took another swig from the bottle. He folded his arms and smiled into the fire.

"So, what happened next?" someone said. "Did he escape?"

"Well," said Robin, "here's where the story gets a little muddled. The fact of the matter is, the authorities didn't want to attempt another execution, and at the same time they wouldn't admit defeat by keeping him in prison. They decided to ship Kingdom to Australia, which first of all allowed them to wash their hands of him completely, and it also served as an effective warning to anyone who might attempt the same trick. What happened after that is pure speculation. We know this much: Kingdom never arrived in Australia. He disappeared shortly after his ship departed. Some suggested it was suicide, but to me, that's preposterous. Why would a man who had survived the gallows deliberately take his own life? Even if the conditions on board were close to unbearable, the man had proven that his instincts for survival were stronger than most.

"Others suggest that he was murdered. This is also highly unlikely. Kingdom was a hero, and not just among the criminal fraternity. His story had spread like wildfire across the country. Songs were sung about him, from popular ballads to children's nursery rhymes. If it was murder, it would have to have been a crime of jealousy, committed by a criminal brave enough to take him on.

"It is my firm belief that Kingdom survived. I don't know how he survived, or what happened to him afterwards. While I'd draw the line at being drawn in by any of the various myths and legends that tell of Kingdom's life in various parts of Europe following his escape from the prison ship, my faith remains in the idea that Kingdom lived a long life. I'd like to think he was happy, too. But that last part is pure speculation on my part."

There is an old fishing expression which sums up the reaction of Robin's audience that evening: *hook, line and sinker.* Their mouths were hanging open in wonder like a row of salmon on a bed of ice.

Of course, the story was total fiction. I'd heard Robin tell it on numerous occasions, and he often changed parts of it as he went along. He made up the names of the characters on the spot. For the judge, he used a different poet every time: Byron, Shelley, Wordsworth. One time, he even called him Seamus Heaney. His reference to Australia was a complete anachronism. Convicts did not begin to be shipped to the country until the later part of the eighteenth century. But no one ever seemed to pull him up on that.

"Anyone else got any gallows stories?" said Robin. "While we're in the morbid mood."

"I heard a story a few years ago," I said, "about a man on death row in America. He was sentenced to be killed in the electric chair, and when it came to the day of his execution, he was asked if he had any last requests. The man said, 'I do indeed. Before I die, I will ask for nothing more than to sing one last song.' The executioners agreed. So the prisoner opened his mouth and sang, *'A million green bottles, hanging on the wall...'*"

No-one laughed, apart from Robin, who slapped himself on the thigh and hollered. A sympathy laugh if ever there was one. He wasn't quite that drunk yet.

"It's a true story," I added, as though that were supposed to make it any funnier.

"So what happened?" someone said.

"What do you mean?" I said.

"Did they let him finish the whole song?"

"I don't know."

So that was the end of that.

"Has anyone heard the story of Vincent Cheem?" said Robin, breaking the awkward silence.

No one had heard that story either. Robin proceeded to give a long and detailed account of the story of Vincent Cheem in his own inimitable style.

Once again, his audience was hooked. They even believed him. They believed the story had actually taken place, in spite of its obvious fantastic elements. By the end of the evening, they were talking about converting to Buddhism.

I didn't attempt to top Robin's performance. There really was no competing. But still, despite my jealousy, I found some comfort in the notion that, entertaining though Robin's version of the Vincent Cheem story was, there remained other, better ways of conveying it.

I came to the decision that night that I would write my own story of Vincent Cheem. It would be the greatest version of the story the world had ever seen. A story that in years to come would be seen as my one true masterpiece.

◘

Greenwich stopped reading for a moment. The story had given him an idea, but he couldn't quite put his finger on what it was. He initially supposed it was some kind of artistic inspiration brought on by the rediscovery of his old work, but it turned out to be something far more practical than that: *the fire.*

The bookcase had made him almost completely immobile, and he'd given up even thinking about struggling free. To attempt to do so would be a waste of energy. As crazy as it sounded, the only way he was going to get out from under the bookcase was to set it alight.

There were obvious risks involved with this plan. He was likely to burn, or choke to death. But if he was going to die anyway, and if setting the bookcase on fire was the only option, he might as well take it.

The cellar door was open, and beyond that, the windows in the kitchen were wide open too. That would relieve him of some of the smoke. The plan was simple: he would lie there until enough of the weight above him had been burned away, and then smash his way through to safety. In theory, it might only take a matter of seconds. The books would go straight up in flames. The question was, would he be able to get out in time? Unfortunately, there was only one way to find out.

His hands were by his sides, so he was able to reach into his pocket for his lighter. When he'd done so, he tried to lift it as high as he could away from his body, pushing it through the mound of books.

Without a second thought, he clicked his finger over the zipper, holding it down to secure the flame.

Straight away, the smoke hit his nostrils.

A second later, his hand made contact with the burning books, and he slammed it back against the floor as hard as he could.

He spluttered as the smoke filled his lungs, and before he knew what was happening his eyes were closed and he was dead to the world.

The manuscript he'd been reading was placed just next to his head and had not yet been caught by the flames.

The manuscript said:

The beauty of the Vincent Cheem story is its simplicity. You could capture the whole thing in a sentence if you wanted. No doubt there is someone, somewhere who has written the story as a haiku.

It is this simplicity that grants the narrative its flexibility. The story can be told within the context of any genre you care to name. When I decided that I would attempt to produce a version of the story myself, as a crime novelist I was naturally inclined toward my own field of expertise. Unfortunately, I was beaten to it by a glorified hack by the name of Claude Lint.

Claude Lint had built up quite a reputation for himself, writing what his marketers liked to call "psychological thrillers", but in reality were little more than shameless festivals of gore and stylised violence, backed up by a tokenistic level of research into police procedures.

Lint was a notorious recluse, and had never been interviewed or even photographed. Now and again, I would come across articles about him by people who ought to know better, debating whether or not his works should be regarded as trash or literature, or somewhere in between. Personally, I would opt for the former.

Lint's novel *Vincent* is arguably and regrettably the most successful version of the Vincent Cheem story yet to be produced. Aside from the ending, the plot is pretty much standard Lint territory: Vincent is a cannibalistic serial killer, who mutilates the corpses of his victims before selecting parts of their bodies to eat. Each of the seven or eight murders in the novel is relayed in meticulously gruesome detail, while the character's motivations for the killings are never satisfactorily explained. As far as the author is concerned, Vincent is a madman, pure and simple. What further explanation is needed?

Eventually, after successfully evading detection by the authorities, Vincent is killed when he inadvertently enters the house of another serial killer, Lint's long-running character Moses Davis. Davis kills Vincent and dumps his body in a derelict cellar, leaving him there to rot. The final passage sees Vincent reincarnated as a maggot, who proceeds to eat his own flesh. Lint's description, as you might expect, leaves little to the imagination.

This tendency to leave little to the imagination is my principle problem with Claude Lint. My gripes have little to do with the graphic violence, although I have to admit, I'm not an admirer of that either. My main objection is that he never offers his readers the opportunity to think.

Now, you might consider this a slightly bitchy reaction, but I wrote to Lint expressing my distaste. While I'll admit there was a certain amount of malice in my intentions, my letter was also a request for information. I was interested to know exactly how he had come across the story, and how many different versions of it he had heard. My thinking was: if I was going to carry out this task properly, I would first of all need to know exactly how other people had done it.

The letter went like this:

Dear Mr Lint,

I'm sure that you are familiar with my work, as I am fairly familiar with yours. Although I am not what you would call a fan, I nonetheless take an interest in your novels, as both an enthusiast and a competitor.

I read your recent novel *Vincent* with interest. I say "with interest" because while I consider your book to be probably one of the worst novels ever written, I am nonetheless fascinated by your choice of source material.

Let's face facts, Claude. Although you appear to have carelessly omitted the mention in your acknowledgements section, Vincent Cheem is not your own creation. He may have been given "the Lint treatment", so to speak, but nonetheless, the central concept is ripped straight from a timeless fable; a story that's been passed down through generations of storytellers, perhaps for hundreds of years. Of course, you are perfectly free to use it within the usual copyright rules, and this is by no means an accusation of plagiarism. The fact that you've butchered a classic is another matter entirely.

As I'm sure you'll already be aware, having conducted your research, there are no clues as to the origins of the Vincent Cheem story. The likelihood is, considering its pseudo-religious nature, that it originated somewhere in Asia. If that is indeed the case, it is probable that the character was not originally called Vincent Cheem. The name was presumably added later as a means of appealing to Western audiences. I should congratulate you on retaining the name yourself. You could easily have changed it to further disguise the source of your inspiration, but as I'm sure you'll agree, the title just feels right somehow.

As the story has developed over time, many people have attempted to retell the story on their own terms, as you have done. This, in many ways, is the point of the story. It adapts itself to suit each individual writer's style.

My enquiry is a simple one: where did you first hear the story of Vincent Cheem, and what was the nature of this version of the story?

Thank you for taking the time to read this letter, and apologies about the sharpness of my critique. I look forward to your response.

Regards,

'Anonymous'

Two weeks later, I received this letter back from Lint:

Dear Mr 'Anonymous',

Allow me to pull you up on a couple of points.

Firstly, you describe *Vincent* as 'probably one of the worst novels ever written'. I am slightly surprised to hear you say this, firstly because you obviously read it all the way through, which begs the question, if a four-hundred-page novel is so awful, why not stop after the first chapter? Secondly, your reaction raises another question: what is so different between my novels and yours?

As you suggest, I am familiar with your work. When it comes to a comparison between our differing approaches to the genre, I can only assume that your objection to my work has something to do with the violent nature of many of my stories. I have often been accused of gratuitous violence. My reaction to this accusation is that yes, my books contain violence for its own sake, because this is the kind of violence that fascinates me. The concept of violence as a means to an end—A kills B in order to inherit B's fortune, or B kills A because A was having an affair with B's wife—is to my mind the stuff of mediocre, generic crime fiction. On the other hand, the idea that men and women can and will commit acts of violence purely to satisfy their own instincts is a far more thought-provoking notion than those standard, painfully logical narratives. Moreover, having read your work, I believe this is a sensibility you also share. We just happen to express our ideas in different styles.

While I wholeheartedly accept the accusation of gratuitous violence, there is another accusation that I reject with equal vigour: *immorality*. You don't simply write about immorality, I am told. *Your books are immoral things. You are an immoral person.* The main reason for this accusation is that I do not appear to condemn the acts of violence depicted in my books.

I'm sure you'll agree that this is a ridiculous concept. We all know that murder is a bad thing. The very idea of saying "murder is a bad thing" is stating the obvious, and if I were to add a postscript at the end of each of my books saying "By the way, murder is a bad thing" I would probably be hit by an even harsher barrage of criticism. You may call me a bad writer if you like, but at least I will never stoop as low as to appear patronising.

I suspect that these accusations stem from the fact that, unlike with your novels, there is no real sense of justice in my work. Bad things happen to good people, and those responsible often get away scot-free. If I have one criticism to make of your work it is this: *you have a twisted sense of justice.*

You may call that a moral statement, but I am merely playing an apparent moralist at his own game. Whenever I read one of your novels, I hear your voice—the voice of the omniscient third-person narrator—passing judgement on the actions he describes. Take your recent novel, in which you have one of your characters arrive home after a particularly hard day at the office, relieving his frustration by kicking the neighbour's cat, only to be savaged to death the following day by a sabre-toothed tiger. What exactly are you trying to say? While I'm sure publicly you would never do anything so unfashionably right wing as to advocate the death penalty, in your fiction you appear to be prescribing death for even the most minor misdemeanour. I'll accept that kicking the neighbour's cat is not a pleasant thing to do, but for a man to have his life taken from him simply for that one act of cruelty is frankly preposterous. It's not even "an eye for an eye" —the cat survived being kicked.

Nonetheless, I will not describe your book as "one of the worst novels ever written". That, my friend, would be childish, and untruthful. In actual fact, I found the novel highly entertaining. I apologise for offering your book, as you might put it, "the Lint treatment". Keep up the good work.

Regards,

Claude Lint

I wrote back with the following:

Dear Mr Lint,

Thank you for your letter. I admit that my description of your novel *Vincent* was a little below the belt. Yes, I read the book all the way through, and yes, I grudgingly admit to having enjoyed it. Your work to me is a guilty pleasure—not because I think you are an immoral writer, but simply because I don't think you have a great deal of artistic integrity.

If it's any excuse, I am still trying to come to terms with the death of my wife. As you suggest, there is no justice in life, and sometimes innocent people die for no reason. I would try to find solace in my writing if only I didn't make a living from writing about death. It is perhaps for this reason that I have decided to write my own version of the Vincent Cheem story, as a means of breaking away from death, if only for a brief time.

You see, my interpretation of the story is that it is not a story about death. It is a story about new life, and perhaps somewhere in there it could be perceived as an alternative salvation narrative. Perhaps my main objection to your version of the story is that you have ignored this positive, life-affirming aspect.

I would be interested to hear your thoughts on this matter.

Regards,

'Anonymous'

Lint replied with the following:

Dear 'Anonymous',

So, you would be "interested to hear my thoughts", would you? Me? A man with no artistic integrity? Why do you care so much about my opinion? I have a better idea—why don't you go fuck yourself?

Regards,

Claude Lint

I wrote back:

Dear Mr Lint,

Apologies for my accusation. I suppose I just need to come to terms with the fact that you sell more books than I do. I know that literature is not meant to be a competition, and I admit that my attitude towards you is rather childish.

By the way, you never answered my question. Where did you first hear the story of Vincent Cheem? I would be genuinely interested to know.

Regards,

'Anonymous'

Lint replied:

Dear 'Anonymous',

I too must offer you an apology. I was having a very bad day when I wrote my previous letter. It's a long story, and you don't need to hear about it. Maybe it will turn into a novel some day. A good novel, I mean. Not like the trash that we churn out. You were right all along, by the way. In a way, I'm disappointed that you apologised. There really was no need. I trust it was an empty apology, which is all I feel I deserve.

In answer to your question, I did not carry out a great deal of research. I have only ever heard one other version of the story of Vincent Cheem. It was told to me by a friend of mine, Robin Carter, on a camping weekend. Robin is a fine storyteller, and is much more worthy of praise than you or I. He writes novels, but fails to get them published. Still, that just goes to prove that only bluffers like us will ever make money from writing. My advice is, if you want a good story, speak to Robin. I believe you know him already?

I hope this is of some help.

Regards,

Claude Lint

◘

Malcolm Greenwich was dreaming. He was dreaming that he was in the middle of an air raid during the Blitz, only it wasn't the Blitz, it was three hundred years into the future, and London was being attacked from the air by ships firing giant laser beams.

He was in a cellar, lying on the ground, as this was the only position in which he could feel safe. If the house was hit, perhaps he could survive if he stayed low enough.

An alarm was going off above him, filling his head with its continuous *beepbeepbeepbeepbeepbeepbeepbeepbeep*, and for a while he was almost hypnotised. It made him forget about the situation he was in, and how close he was to death.

He lifted his head, and realised there was somebody else in the room. A man was sitting on a chair in the corner, but Greenwich couldn't make out his face in the darkness.

"How long have you been sitting there?" said Greenwich.

"As long as you've been lying there," said the man.

"How long have I been lying here?" said Greenwich.

"Does it matter?" said the man.

"I suppose not," said Greenwich. "We're going to die, aren't we?"

"You don't know that for certain," said the man.

"Do you believe in miracles?" said Greenwich.

"It doesn't matter whether I believe in miracles or not," said the man. "The question is, are miracles going to happen today?"

"Who are you?" said Greenwich.

"Does it matter?" said the man.

"We're going to die, aren't we?" said Greenwich.

"Yes, we are," said the man.

They paused for a while, listening to the *beepbeepbeepbeep*ing of the alarm.

"Any last requests?" said the man.

"That's not funny," said Greenwich. "We're going to die."

"That's the whole point," said the man. "If we know that's going to happen, we don't have any social obligations anymore. We can do anything, or say anything, and not have to worry about the consequences. We can reveal our deepest, darkest secrets, and it won't matter."

"Go on, then," said Greenwich.

"What do you mean?" said the man.

"Tell me your secrets. Something you've never told anyone."

"I wasn't talking about me. I'm just a figment of your imagination."

"Really?"

"Why do you think you can't see me properly? I'm barely here at all. Characterisation was never your strong point."

"So if I reveal my deepest, darkest secret, I'd effectively just be speaking to myself?"

"Maybe you have to admit it to yourself. Maybe that's why I'm here."

"OK," said Greenwich, "are you ready for it?"

"Of course."

"OK."

"Well, then?"

"OK," said Greenwich. "I killed someone, once. Are you happy?"

"Are you?"

"About killing someone? Of course I'm not happy."

"It feels good to say it out loud, though, doesn't it? After all these years? Try telling me some more, see how it feels."

"OK," said Greenwich. "This person that I killed, they were very special to me. I didn't realise or appreciate it at the time, but I loved them. I really did. And then after it happened, I suppose I had a kind of breakdown. I wrote a short story called *The Life and Death of Vincent Cheem*, which was supposed to be a kind of confession, but no one seemed to realise that that's what it was, least of all the relevant authorities. People just thought it was a good story—maybe my best. The fact that I appeared to be confessing to a murder was all part of the fun—an artistic in-joke. But it was all true. I changed the names, and a few of the details, but the basic story—the fact that I killed someone—I wasn't making that up. It actually happened."

"Do you feel better now?"

Greenwich had nothing more to say.

He just lay there, listening to the alarm, drifting off to sleep.

Back in the real world, he was lying in his cellar underneath a bookcase in the middle of a cloud of smoke.

The manuscript sat next to his head.

The manuscript said:

I tried to conduct as much research as I could about Vincent Cheem, but the results were few and far between. I sent letters out to as many writers as I knew, asking them if they were familiar with the story. As is only to be expected, some had heard it, others hadn't. Most couldn't remember where it was that they'd come across it, but the story rang a bell somehow. One writer sent me a copy of a story he'd seen in a magazine, about an alcoholic who died and was resurrected as a maggot. The character did not have a name, but it was clearly a version of Vincent Cheem.

The story was possibly the most heartbreaking piece of prose I had ever laid eyes on. I wept from start to finish, while at the same time marvelling at the writer's ability to use this resurrection story as a metaphor for the character's dependence on drink. It was a vision of an addiction that literally ate away at its victim.

The story had been written anonymously. I wrote to the magazine to see if they could give me any more information on the author, but they were unable to help. Perhaps it was better for me not to know. The story had clearly been written by someone who'd experienced addiction first hand. Perhaps the writer was dead as well. I hoped not, but still, I resisted the temptation to dig any deeper.

You might expect such an affecting version of the Vincent Cheem story to put me off writing my one myself, but no, quite the opposite. I'd long since given up on the idea of there being a perfect version of the story. There was no Platonic ideal. There were just different versions of the same thing.

I went to visit Robin to show him the magazine I'd found.

We sat in his study. I had a cup of tea, while he drank a glass of brandy. I began to wonder if Robin had a problem with drinking himself. It was eleven o'clock in the morning.

"This is excellent," he said, "I like it a lot. And written anonymously as well, that adds that extra dose of mystery to it, don't you think?"

"I don't know," I said. "I'm not sure about people who write things anonymously. There seems something a little dishonest about it."

"What about people who write under pseudonyms?" he said.

"Same thing, I suppose."

"But what's in a name?"

"You're right." I smiled. "You're always right, aren't you? I'm not sure how you do it."

I was flattering him, of course. Robin wasn't always right, and he knew that himself.

Take his writing career, or lack of it, as an example. Robin had written a trilogy of fantasy novels, which were unpublished, and remain so to this day, despite the fact that the second volume in the trilogy, *The Wind*, is probably the greatest novel ever written. I read the whole five hundred pages in one weekend, and it would be no exaggeration to say that it changed my life. Robin gave it to me shortly after the death of my wife, a time when I was suffering a considerable level of inner pain, but after reading the novel it was as though somehow my soul had been restored, alongside my faith in human nature. As with all the best of Robin's work, the beauty of the book lies in the author's ability to make you believe what you are reading. Somehow you are made to feel that this is not just something that happened, but it's something that *is happening*, as you read it, despite it being set in a mythical place and time, and despite the fact that it's only a book. As a writer, I would have happily killed for his gift.

The trouble is, the first part of the trilogy, *The Mist*, is virtually impossible to read. There is very little plot, or characterisation, or any real form of entertainment. *The Mist* basically serves as a kind of explanation for parts two and three. Unfortunately, while the novel serves an important purpose, because of its impenetrability, no publisher would dream of touching either the novel or the trilogy. I had suggested that Robin try to publish the second part as a stand-alone novel, but the problem was you had to read the first part in order for the second part to make sense. Worse still, neither of us could see a way of making the first part any more readable. It had to be written in that particular way.

The third part of the trilogy, *The Rain*, is fine as fantasy novels go. It reads well, but it often reminded me of why I'm not a particular fan of the genre. It's not a patch on the second part, but again, the book is necessary in order to round off the story properly.

This was the kind of writer that Robin was. He had flashes of genius, but he lacked consistency. Still, it's better than having the consistency but not the genius. There was something quite tragic about it, but aside from his heavy drinking, it never seemed to get Robin down. He lived in a large house, and never needed to worry about money, despite his apparent lack of an income. I'd always assumed that he had wealthy parents, although I had no real evidence to back that up. Robin never spoke about his family.

"So, how's your version of the story coming along?" he said.

"Not bad," I said. "I'm thinking of making it into a kind of political allegory. Something about the conflict between the individual and the collective."

"And how does that fit in with Vincent Cheem?" he said.

"Well," I said, "I think the basic story will run something like this: Cheem is a complete individualist. He's self-serving, self-centred, and entirely sucked in by the false hopes of capitalism. I haven't figured out how he dies yet—maybe there's a stock market crash, and he's bankrupted and dies out on the street, or maybe he makes so much money that he gets crushed to death by a pile of his own possessions."

"You like it when they get crushed to death, don't you?"

"Well, it's an effective metaphor for the state the character is in. Plus it serves its purpose, because the whole point of the story is that Vincent Cheem dies. So once he's dead, as we all know, he gets reincarnated as the maggot, and when he's in that state, he can feel himself working for the first time in his life as part of a dedicated group. He's aware of all his other maggot brothers and sisters, striving together towards a common goal, and it's at this point that Vincent finds true happiness. I know it sounds a bit corny when you put it in those basic terms, but if I write it well enough, it could be great."

"It certainly sounds interesting," said Robin. "I can't wait to read it."

Spurred on by Robin's enthusiasm, I went home that afternoon and wrote the whole thing from start to finish. It was three o'clock in the morning by the time I'd completed it. I poured myself a drink and read the short story back to myself, quite taken aback by my own sophistication.

Perhaps, I thought, I *would never need to write another bad crime novel again. I could use my remaining years in the pursuit of serious literature.*

It was as though I had rediscovered the joys of writing, after years of simply going through the motions. My life had encountered a number of unexpected turning points, and this, apparently, was another. Maybe the best.

I slept fitfully that night, still excited about my achievement.

The following morning, I took a copy round to Robin's house, and showed it to him.

Robin seemed in a particularly bad mood, but I didn't want to question him on it. He looked as though he hadn't slept all night, and when I rang the bell, he half-heartedly called "Come in" instead of answering.

I came through to his study to find him sitting at his desk with a blank piece of paper in his typewriter. I got the impression he'd been sitting there for some time.

When I offered him the story he took it and read it, not with a lack of enthusiasm as such, but with a completely blank expression, offering no clues as to his state of mind.

"It's good," he said when he'd finished. "I like the description. I think you'll have trouble getting it published, though."

"Oh," I said. "Why's that?"

"Because it's already been done," he said.

He reached into his desk drawer, and pulled out a magazine.

"I'm sorry," he said, "I should've showed you this yesterday. I thought your idea sounded familiar, but I wasn't quite sure what to say."

He handed me the magazine. It was open at the right page.

I found myself looking at a short story called *The Life and Death of Vincent Cheem*, by Robin Carter.

I could see as soon as I started reading that this story was almost an exact replica of my own. Here and there, a word or phrase was different, but...

"What's going on?" I said.

"We've written the same story," he said, simply.

"You're not surprised?"

"It happens more often than you'd think, actually," said Robin. "It's more likely to happen when the two writers know each other. They develop a kind of psychic link—it's not uncommon. It's a collective unconscious thing."

"Codswallop," I said. "I've never heard of anything more ridiculous." I scrunched the magazine up in my hand and waved it in front of his face. "Yes, it's a good trick, I'll give you that! I don't know how you managed to pull it off, but you're playing games with me, Robin, and I don't like it! I'm not going to stand for it!"

"I'm sorry," he said, "but I really haven't being trying to trick you. You sat down and wrote that story of your own free will. I may have given you the idea, but it still came from you. You could say we did it together."

I head was wagging like a tail. I sat down, not sure about what to think.

"So, when did you write this?" I said.

"About a year ago. I had this idea for a story about a man who dies and gets reincarnated as a maggot. I called him Vincent Cheem because I liked the name, but I had to play around and experiment a little while I tried to find a suitable way of writing the story—just like you did, I suppose."

"OK, now I know you're hoodwinking me," I said. "The story of Vincent Cheem is hundreds of years old. You didn't make it up, it's been passed down from generation to ..."

"No, it hasn't," he said. "I only said it had, because that was all part of the story I was telling."

"So you just made it up?" I said.

"Yes," he said.

"So, all those details about no one being sure about the origins, maybe it was Eastern, blah blah blah, that was all ..."

"Fiction," he said. "I'm a fiction writer."

"You're a *liar*!" I shouted.

"What's the difference?" he said.

Robin delivered that last line with such insufferable smugness that I became disgusted by his presence.

"What's the matter with you?" I said. "Are you drunk?"

"Sure," he said. "Why not?"

"Why do you feel the need to drink so much?"

"I just had a bad day," he said. "It's a long story, and you don't need to hear about it. Maybe it will turn into a novel some day. A good novel, I mean. Not like the trash that we churn out."

"What the fuck are you doing?" I said. "Have you been going through my things?"

Robin seemed genuinely upset by the accusation, which enraged me still further. "What do you mean?" he said.

"You know what I mean," I said. "Why did you say that? I know that you know Claude Lint, he told me so himself. Is he part of your little game as well?"

"I'm not playing games with you," he said.

143

My hands were clutching him by the shirt, and he was slapping me, trying to get me off him. "You are!" I was shouting, "You fucking are, and you know it!"

I grabbed something from on the desk. I didn't know what it was that I'd picked up, but it turned out to be a wire coathanger. Before I knew what I was doing, I was wrapping it over his head, lifting him against the door and hooking the hanger over the frame.

I stood back, appalled, as he hung, suffocating before me, his feet tap-dancing in the air.

I didn't move.

I'd written about the experience so many times, but it was nothing like the real thing. I enjoyed writing about murder, but I never liked to dwell on the subject. I usually summed it all up in a few simple sentences. As I stood there, I could hear my own voice, narrating the scene from the comfort of my writing desk:

I knew he was dead, and there was nothing I could do about it.

Robin was dead, and I had killed him.

I couldn't get out of the room without crawling underneath his feet.

I settled instead for climbing out of the window.

◘

Greenwich opened his eyes and broke straight into a coughing fit. With each cough came another spasm of pain, and the fact that he had a large bookcase resting on his chest was not helping matters.

He could hardly see because of the smoke, but he could tell that it was clearing. The fire must have gone out almost as soon as it had started.

He stopped coughing.

The smoke alarm was going *beepbeepbeepbeepbeepbeepbeepbeep*.

He tried to move, but it was no good, he was still trapped.

He had a throbbing pain in his hand where the fire had got him.

He was still there, though. He supposed that being so low down was what had saved him in the end.

Setting fire to the books had clearly been a stupid idea. He would have to think of another plan. This wasn't over yet.

His house was miles from any town, and he knew it would be unlikely that a passer by would hear the alarm and come to his rescue. It wasn't impossible, but he certainly wasn't going to lie there and wait for some Good Samaritan.

The smoke cleared a little more, and once again he noticed the manuscript that was sitting next to his head. Most of it had been burned by the fire, but somehow, the last page had survived.

He looked up, and read:

The following day, the report came on the news.

It wasn't quite the report I'd been expecting.

The popular crime novelist Claude Lint has been found dead in his home in London.

I turned up the volume to hear if I'd heard the name correctly.

Lint was most famous for his novels featuring the fictional serial killer Moses Davis and although many considered his books distasteful he nonetheless had millions of devoted fans throughout the world. Lint lived a reclusive life, and was never publicly interviewed. He even wrote under a pseudonym. He was known to friends and family as Robin Carter. In a gruesome scene reminiscent of one of his books, Lint was discovered hanging in his study, having apparently taken his own life. It is thought that Lint had been drinking heavily prior to the incident.

I don't know what else I can tell you apart from that. I gave up trying to write my own version of the Vincent Cheem story and continued to knock out bad crime novels. I moved to a house in the country, where I live alone, just me and my work. You could say that Robin, or Claude, or should I call him "Anonymous", had died for fiction. I can only try to honour him by living for it. Perhaps one day I will write something that people will believe in rather than just read, although in a sense, that's entirely out of my control.

I suspect that if you go out looking for inspiration you aren't going to find it. Like friends or lovers, inspiration arrives uninvited, and is gone again just as quickly.

As I say, I'm not looking to make my millions from writing this piece. I'm just a criminal trying to clear his conscience.

In case you were wondering, it hasn't worked.

So much for the power of the pen.

◘

Greenwich stopped reading and laid his head back.

So much for the power of the pen.

Was that really the last line? This was supposed to be his masterpiece. He'd actually killed a man in order to produce it, and in the end he sounded so defeatist.

He could hardly believe they were his own words. He realised he'd spent so much time being angry and frustrated in the past. All those wasted years when he could've been enjoying himself.

He couldn't remember writing it now and had no idea what had been going through his mind at the time. It was as though he were reading someone else's words.

He couldn't explain why, but somehow the story had given him strength.

He knew how to get out from under the bookcase now. It was easy. It was simply a matter of concentration.

Greenwich closed his eyes and focused. He channelled all his remaining energy into his right foot. On the count of three, he told himself, his leg would be all-powerful.

He counted to three and kicked. The bookcase jumped up from on top of him. He held his leg up at a right angle, and found that he could move his arms again. He swept off the charred volumes that covered his torso and reached up to touch the shelves. He pushed the case back up to an upright position and carried on lying there.

He could breathe again. He took a long draught of air before getting to his feet.

There's a story in here somewhere, he thought, and then found himself laughing. The laughter stung his chest, but he couldn't stop. It had taken the experience of nearly being killed to finally make him see the funny side.

He went upstairs to the kitchen to make himself something to eat. He was starving, and he had no idea how long he'd been down there. In a way, he didn't want to know.

He took the batteries out of the smoke alarm, relieved at the sudden silence.

His plan was to have some food, change his clothes and then go to the hospital.

He ate a sandwich, and decided it was time to get some fresh air.

Something wasn't quite right. He couldn't quite put his finger on what it was. He'd almost died today, but there was a part of him that felt disappointed that he hadn't. Surely that was crazy. Perhaps the smoke had made him slightly drunk.

He stepped out into the garden and looked up at the sky. He hadn't even realised it was daytime. He wandered around for a while, occasionally chuckling to himself for no apparent reason. He imagined the news reports if he'd actually stayed down there. *In a gruesome scene reminiscent of one of his books …* Journalists loved it when life imitated art. Writers loved it when journalists called them artists.

Not really thinking where he was going, Greenwich opened the garden gate and stepped out into the narrow country lane.

He stood there for some time, looking at the hills, wondering what it was he was missing.

He was knocked out of his trance by a noise to his left.

He turned, and was surprised to see a truck heading towards him. The driver obviously hadn't expected anyone to be standing there, and had not reduced his speed.

The two of them realised at the same time, and both darted out of the way. Greenwich dived for the side of the road, and the truck driver swerved to avoid him.

Greenwich hit the ground and looked up to see the truck colliding with the dry stone wall on the opposite side of the lane.

He jumped to his feet and ran towards the truck to see if the driver was OK.

A second later he was knocked to the ground. The back doors of the truck had flown open with the impact, and its contents came flying out.

Greenwich was lying on his back again, helpless, as the cargo piled up on top of him.

The truck had been delivering coathangers. Thousands and thousands of wire hangers, stacked on top of each other, their combined weight heavy enough to crush a man to death.

The front wheels of the truck had gone up on to the wall, tipping a whole mountain of hangers out on to the ground.

The driver stumbled out of the cab and crouched down to see if he could still bend his legs.

It was OK, nothing was broken. He was shaken up, though.

He looked around for the person he'd almost hit, but there was no one to be seen. The man had obviously run off as soon as he realised he'd caused an accident. The pedestrian version of a hit and run.

That's gratitude for you, the driver thought. *You almost end up killing yourself to avoid colliding with someone and they don't even stick around to see if you're alright.*

He remembered a story a friend had told him once about a similar situation. At the time he'd hardly believed it. He thought no one would've been that selfish.

It just goes to show, he thought. *There really are bad people in the world.*

The driver made a call from his mobile, alerting the emergency services. He knew they might be a while, considering how far he was into the countryside.

There was a house just beside him, so he knocked on the door to see if there was anyone there. No one replied, but he got the impression he was being ignored. It smelt like they were having a barbecue out the back.

He returned to the truck, thinking it best to alert any oncoming traffic of the blockage he'd caused. He sat down on the mountain of coathangers and breathed a sigh of relief.

At least no one was hurt.

THE NATURE OF HUMAN HAPPINESS BY F.R. PSEUDOVICH
With an Introduction and Notes by V.W. Tippington

A PHILISTINE PUBLICATION

Also available by F.R. Pseudovich from Philistine Books

Everyman For Himself
Dissecting Humanity
Humanity In Crisis
One Small Step For Man
Man Oh Man!
Man In Discussion
   Humanity: A Users Guide
      Humanity, Vanity And The Question of Sanity
         Whoops There Goes Another Rubber Tree Plant, But No-one
         Was Around To See It (A Study of Humanity)
   and   Blackcurrant Flavour Chewits (A Memoir)

Introduction

As the fifth anniversary of F.R. Pseudovich's death draws close at hand, it is perhaps time to reflect on this, his final philosophical work. I use the term "reflect" rather than reassess, as although numerous assessments have been made of *The Nature of Human Happiness*, there is little in the way of a critical consensus. Are we to view this strikingly slim volume as a swansong, or (as one reviewer would have it) "the incoherent ramblings of a dying genius"? Is it a culmination of a lifetime's ideas and reading laid down finally in a concise and digestible form, or is it, as G.W. Groomspek pronounced prior to its initial publication, "a glorified self-help book"?

Questions of Pseudovich's validity aside, the subject upon which the philosopher's scholars are perhaps most equally divided is the author's intentions in writing this book. Is it, as some speculate, an unfinished work—the beginnings of a masterpiece, cut short by his terrible illness? Or does the text appear as Pseudovich intended it—the completely blank "Conclusion" section a bold and triumphant demonstration that there *are* no conclusions to be made?

The author's death came as a devastating surprise to all concerned. The emotional impact has been doubled by the fact that the body is yet to be traced. Only Pseudovich and his doctors were aware of his condition at the time of his writing. Both his family and his publishing company, Philistine Books—rumoured correctly to have paid a one-and-a-half-thousand dollar advance—were kept entirely in the dark. This text, therefore, is the only indication we have as to the state of the philosopher's mind in his final days.

In order to gain a fuller understanding of this highly complex individual, however, we must go back further in time—not simply to scrutinise his indispensable body of work, but to examine his life. What, we ask ourselves, was Pseudovich really *like*? It is difficult to say. *Blackcurrant Flavour Chewits* is, of course, an essential guide in this area. What are also useful, however, are the accounts made by those who knew him. I remember the first time I went to see Pseudovich lecture. What struck me that day was not the man's ability to connect with the audience, impressive though that was—I even forget now the content of the lecture itself. What struck me was his overwhelming sincerity. In approaching him nervously afterwards, hoping for a little further insight (as well as a signature for my copy of *One Small Step For Man*), I now recall not the words that passed between us, but those large, inviting eyes, that warm handshake, and that look on his face that indicated when he said it was a bit cloudy today he *really meant* it was a bit cloudy today.

The *Nature of Human Happiness* is a work that has grown very much out of this sincerity. Instilled in every line of this mighty text is the naked honesty of Keats or Wordsworth, coupled with the intensity of Nietzsche and the attention to detail of Sigmund Freud. Comparisons with his 1,000-page magnum opus, *Humanity: A User's Guide*, are entirely justified, in that while several critics viewed the extensive text as a general overview of the concepts Pseudovich had already cultivated in his previous works (as B.H. Willowfoot tagged it, *F.R. Pseudovich: A Users Guide*), it was in fact a further development, and in many ways a conscious deviation from his previous work. In much the same way, *The Nature of Human Happiness* is a *further* further development, and one perhaps that makes the great man's tragic death ever more upsetting. What, we ask ourselves, would Pseudovich have written had he lived?

The question of the unusual length of this final work continues to haunt us. Pseudovich's exhaustive research (which led him to sell his house and circumvent the globe from one tropical paradise to another—a mark of true dedication) would indeed suggest a more substantial text. I, however, subscribe unapologetically to the school of thought that insists on *The Nature of Human Happiness* as a "finished" work. Pseudovich's assertion that "this is all [we] need to know" confirms this. What emerges in these pages is not incoherence, but near-perfect clarity. Not only is this a complete work, it is perhaps the most complete work by any major philosopher in the last quarter-century. While the text includes such cultural citations as *Columbo* and The Jackson Five, the misinterpretation of these references as unwelcome distractions to an essentially "intellectual" argument has marred the assessments of many critics. Let us not forget that, aside from his love–hate relationship with the modern world and its media, Pseudovich is perhaps the greatest purveyor, alive or dead, of "*truth*" in its purest form.

V.W.T.

Chapter 1

Look, this is all you need to know, OK? You want a deconstruction of human happiness, here it is. 'Cos I've travelled halfway across the world, and what, in "real" terms, have I got to show for it? If I've learned one thing from this whole experience it's that you can't create happiness out of thin air and traveller's cheques.

People constantly question me—that's why I decided to write this book in the first place. What *is* human happiness, they ask me: where does it come from and how, *how*—this is the important one—how do I find it?

The problem with so many of the people I come across in the academic field is that they wish to seek out the *nature* of human happiness, as if having isolated certain chemicals in the brain and carried out certain sociological studies they're automatically destined to become content themselves. (Note my implication that happiness and contentment are the same thing—this has not escaped me either.)

So where do we start looking? Do we look to the Canon? Do we seek out Kydmaswrroliss? Are we really to blame it on the boogie?

What I realise now is what has taken me a lifetime to realise —as although I've spent my life saying it, I never really believed or understood it. It's only now that I'm close to death that the true flexibility of human perception becomes clear. Is it our role as seekers of the truth to be objective in our approaches?

Of course it isn't. Fuck truth. Fuck anyone who seeks it.

Sorry—one more thing, sir ...

Nothing.

CONCLUSION

INDEX

academic field, 1
appreciate, 1
blame, 1
boogie, 1
chemicals, 1
contentment, 1
deconstruction, 1
flexibility, 1
fuck, 1
happiness, 1
Kydmaswrroliss, 1
nature, 1
objective, 1
"real", 1
sociological, 1
sorry, 1

NOTES

Canon: There is a debate over whether Pseudovich's capitalisation of "Canon" refers to the body of work regarded as the most significant in the field of philosophy—what he earlier referred to as "the giants on whose shoulders my heels are happy to dig" —or if "Canon" it is a playfully misspelt reference to warfare. (See Pseudovich's chapter "War and Sartre's God-Shaped Hole" in *Dissecting Humanity*.)

"Certain Sociological Studies": This is believed to be a subtle jibe at N.K. Howler's book *The Pursuit of Pleasure*—a study of hedonism and alternative living which Pseudovich considered "a self-indulgent and yet highly subtle way of patronising the lower orders".

"Close to Death": This is, of course, the only written evidence of Pseudovich's terminal illness. As one who knew him, my message to any conspiracy theorists is to view this line as exactly that: *evidence,* indisputable evidence that Pseudovich was a dying man. Are we to ignore the recent newspaper reports of forged passports and mislaid medical records? I do not suggest that we ignore them— rather that we hold them up as evidence themselves, not of Pseudovich's life or death, but of the increasing tabloidisation, not merely of the broadsheet press but of Western thought in general.

Kydmaswrroliss: There is no record of this word in any written language, and it is believed to be of Pseudovich's own devising. The term is widely regarded as a reference to Pseudovich's concept of a quasi-spiritual Nirvana. It has also been suggested by G.N. Frink, amongst others, that Kydmaswrroliss is an invented figure from the history of mythology—a figure Pseudovich planned to use later in further illustrating his ideas.

    (In the interests of a balanced commentary, however, I must also make mention of the fact that a number of cynics have identified "Kydmaswrroliss" to be an anagram of "world kiss my arse".)

Frank Burton

ND - #0506 - 270225 - C0 - 229/152/13 - PB - 9781907133015 - Gloss Lamination